MW00897624

The Hollow Tree and Deep Woods Book

Albert Bigelow Paine

ISBN: 1979002940

ISBN-13: 978-1979002943

Table of Contents

THE LITTLE LADY AND THE STORY TELLER...4

    THE READER IS INTRODUCED TO THEM 4

THE HOLLOW TREE PEOPLE..4

    THE LITTLE LADY IS INTRODUCED TO THE 'COON, THE 'POSSUM AND THE OLD BLACK CROW..4

A JOKE ALL AROUND 9

    ABOUT HOLLOW TREE PEOPLE AND THEIR WAYS...9

SOME NEW ACQUAINTANCES..12

    THE LITTLE LADY IS INTRODUCED TO MR. JACK RABBIT DURING A VERY EXCITING EXPERIENCE WITH MR. DOG. THE FIRST ADVENTURE OF JACK RABBIT.................................12

MR. RABBIT'S BIG DINNER 17

    MR. JACK RABBIT ENTERTAINS THE HOLLOW TREE PEOPLE. AN UNWELCOME GUEST ARRIVES CAUSING SOME EXCITEMENT 17

THE CROW'S COMPANY 25

    MR. CROW GIVES A SUPPER TO MR. DOG, ACCORDING TO PROMISE.......................25

THE FIRST MOON STORY 30

    A STORY IN WHICH MR. 'COON TELLS MR. 'POSSUM AND MR. RABBIT SOMETHING ABOUT THE MOON 30

THE SECOND MOON STORY 34

    MR. 'POSSUM HAS SOMETHING TO SAY ABOUT THE MOON WHICH SHEDS NEW LIGHT ON THE SUBJECT 34

ON THE EDGE OF THE WORLD 37

    MR. RABBIT HAS SOMETHING TO SAY ABOUT THE MOON, DURING WHICH HE EXPLAINS THE SPOTS ON IT 37

THE FIRST PIG STORY...41

    MR. CROW SPENDS A SOCIAL EVENING WITH MR. DOG 41

THE SECOND PIG STORY..43

    MR. DOG TELLS OF ANOTHER RUNAWAY WHO HAS A STRANGE ADVENTURE 43

MR. DOG TAKES LESSONS IN DANCING 46

    JACK RABBIT PLAYS ONE MORE JOKE ON MR. DOG 46

MR. RABBIT'S UNWELCOME COMPANY 51

    MR. POLECAT MAKES A MORNING CALL AND MR. DOG DROPS IN 51

HOW MR. DOG GOT EVEN 52

    THE FOREST FRIENDS PREPARE FOR A MAY PARTY AND ARRANGE FOR A QUIET TIME 52

HOW MR. DOG GOT EVEN 56

    THE SURPRISE OF MR. RABBIT AND OTHERS..56

THE LITTLE LADY'S VACATION AND HER RETURN 63

THE STORY OF THE C. X. PIE 63

    MR. CROW PLANS AN APRIL FIRST PARTY AND PREPARES A SURPRISE FOR THE OCCASION ...63

THE STORY OF THE C. X. PIE 71

    MR. CROW'S PARTY AND THE OPENING OF THE PIES 71

THE STORY OF THE C. X. PIE 77

    WHAT HAPPENS TO MR. CROW AND HIS PIE 77

MR. RABBIT EXPLAINS 80

    AN EASTER STORY...80

MR. TURTLE'S THUNDER STORY 84

    THE WAY OF THE FIRST THUNDER AND LIGHTNING 84

MR. TURTLE'S THUNDER STORY..86

    FATHER STORM'S PLAN AND HOW IT WORKED 86

A RAIN IN THE NIGHT 91

    A WINDOW THAT WASN'T CLOSED, AND WHO CLOSED IT 91

A DEEP WOODS FISHING PARTY...93

    AN ADVENTURE WITH MR. DOG AND A VERY LARGE FISH 93

THE HOLLOW TREE INN 96

    THE THREE FRIENDS GO INTO BUSINESS 96

THE HOLLOW TREE INN 98

    WHAT HAPPENS TO MR. DOG 98

MR. 'POSSUM EXPLAINS 103

    HOW UNCLE SILAS TRIED TO PLEASE AUNT MELISSY 103

THE HOLLOW TREE POETRY CLUB..107

    MR. CROW PLANS AN ENTERTAINMENT FOR THE FOREST PEOPLE 107

AROUND THE WORLD AND BACK AGAIN 115

CHRISTMAS AT THE HOLLOW TREE INN...120

    THE STORY TELLER TOLD THE LAST HOLLOW TREE STORY ON CHRISTMAS EVE. IT WAS SNOWING OUTSIDE, AND THE LITTLE LADY WAS WONDERING HOW IT WAS IN THE FAR DEEP WOODS 120

GOOD-BYE TO THE LITTLE LADY 126

    WHAT SHE WISHES AND WHAT THE STORY TELLER SAYS 126

THE READER IS INTRODUCED TO THEM

In the House of Many Windows which stands in a large city and is sometimes called a "flat" by people who, because they are grown up, do not know any better, live the Little Lady and the Story Teller.

The Little Lady is four years old, going on five, and is fond of stories. This makes her and the Story Teller good friends. They mostly sit in the firelight after supper, and while the Little Lady is being undressed they tell each other all that has happened since morning. Then the Little Lady looks into the fire and says:—

"Now, tell me a story."

Sometimes she wants a new story. Sometimes one of the old ones, which must be told always the same, because the Little Lady, like a good many grown up people, does not care for new and revised editions, but wants the old stories in the old words, that sound real and true. Sometimes the Story Teller forgets or improves on his plots, but the Little Lady never forgets and never fails to set the Story Teller right.

THE HOLLOW TREE PEOPLE

THE LITTLE LADY IS INTRODUCED TO THE 'COON, THE 'POSSUM AND THE OLD BLACK CROW

When the Story Teller came home last night the Little Lady had a great deal to tell him. During the afternoon she had built in one corner of the sitting room a house for her three dolls, with a separate room for each. Of course, the house was not a house at all, but only a plan on the floor made with blocks and books. At one side she had laid out a large parlor room, where her family of three—Hettie, Annabelle and the Rubber Boy—could meet together and talk.

"Why," said the Story Teller, "that reminds me of the Crow, the 'Coon and the 'Possum."

"What did they do? Tell me that story," commanded the Little Lady, promptly forgetting her day's work and pulling the Story Teller toward his chair.

The Story Teller stirred the fire and looked into the blaze a moment, thinking. The Little Lady climbed up into his lap and waited. She was used to the Story Teller.

"Tell it," she said, presently.

So then he told her the story of the three friends.

Once upon a time in the far depths of the Big Deep Woods there was a big hollow tree, with three big hollow branches. In one of these there lived a 'Coon, in another a 'Possum and in the third a Big Black Crow.

"But crows don't live in hollow trees," said the Little Woman, who happened to be passing.

"This one did," replied the Story Teller. "I suppose styles have changed some since then."

The hollow tree below was rather dark, so they all used it for a parlor, and only met in there now and then, to dust off their things, or when company came.

Now, the Crow and the 'Coon and the 'Possum were all very fond of good living and mostly of the same things. They were good friends, too, and they often made plans to catch young chickens and other game and carried them out together. Between trips they would sit in their doors and pass the time of day across to each other, just like folks.

Well, one winter, about two weeks after New Year's, it came on to snow in the woods where the hollow tree was, and it snowed, and it snowed, and it snowed.

This was long before sleds or skates, and when big snows always came up over people's windows and snowed them in. And this is what happened to the Crow and the 'Coon and the 'Possum. They were snowed in!

Well, they rather liked it at first, for they had a good deal left over from New Year's dinner, and they used to get together down stairs in the parlor and spread lunch and pitch the bones under the table and talk and tell stories and wonder how long the snow would last.

4

ROCKED ON PURPOSE TO THINK ABOUT IT.

But they never counted on its lasting half so long as it did. Every day they would look out of an upstairs window that they had, to see if the storm wasn't over. And every day it was just the same, and there was no sign of clearing up. Then they began to get scared, for their cupboards were nearly empty, and there was no chance to catch any more game. At last every scrap was gone, and there wasn't a thing to eat in the house.

LOOKED IN QUITE A WHILE,
THINKING.

The 'Possum went to bed and pulled up the covers and tried to sleep so he would forget it. The 'Coon sat up in a rocking chair and rocked on purpose to think about it, for he was a great hand to plan, and he thought mebbe he could work it out some way. The Crow didn't do either, but walked about his house, picking up first one thing and then another, as people do sometimes when they don't do anything else. But the Crow was luckier than most people who do that, for by and by he picked up quite a big paper sack with something in it. Then he untied it and looked into it quite a while, thinking. It was more than half full of corn meal, and pretty soon he remembered that he had carried it off once when he was passing Mr. Man's pantry window, not because he wanted it, but because he was a crow, and crows carry off anything that isn't too big, whether they want it or not. Then he hunted around some more and found another sack with some flour in it that he had picked up once in the same way. Then he found some little bags of pepper and salt and a lump of butter.

"My!" said the Little Lady, "but he'd carried off a lot of things!"

6

THE 'POSSUM JUMPED STRAIGHT UP IN BED.

Yes, crows always do, and hide them that way. Well, he didn't say anything, but he slipped down stairs and gathered up some of the chicken bones under the table and some pieces of bark and sticks, and brought them up to his own part of the house and shut the door. Then he kindled a little fire in the stove with the sticks and opened his outside door a crack and got a skillet full of snow and put it on, and when the snow melted he dropped in the chicken bones and let them stew, and then a little of the flour and some pepper and salt and stirred it, and he had some nice gravy.

By and by the 'Possum and 'Coon smelt it cooking and thought it came from a farm house, and the 'Possum turned over twice and thought of everything he had ever heard of to make people go to sleep, and the 'Coon rocked harder and harder.

Then Mr. Crow poured the gravy into a bowl and set it back on the stove to keep warm while he stirred up some of the cornmeal in some more melted snow, with a little pinch of salt and a little piece of the butter. When it was all stirred good he put it into the skillet and patted it down, and when it was baked nice and brown on both sides it was as good a Johnnie cake as you ever tasted.

He laughed to himself a minute and then he slipped down stairs again and set the table. He put on the bowl of gravy in the centre and cut the Johnnie cake in three pieces. Then he called out as loud as he could:—

"Come to dinner!"

"DROP IN AGAIN TO-MORROW,"
SAID THE CROW.

The 'Possum jumped straight up in bed and then lay down again quick, for he thought the Crow was playing a joke on him, which he was, though not the kind he thought. The 'Coon jumped, too, and then went to rocking again, for he thought the same thing. So Mr. Crow opened the 'Possum's door quick and the 'Coon's door quick and let the smell of the nice chicken gravy go right up into their rooms. Then he laughed out loud and called again:—

"Come to dinner while it's hot!"

And down they came, for they couldn't stand that smell. But when they saw the Johnnie cake they thought it was a joke again, for they had never seen any before and didn't know what it was like.

"Dip in and try," said the Crow, and he broke off a piece of his cake and dipped it in the bowl of gravy and began to eat it. So then the 'Possum broke off a piece of his Johnnie cake and dipped it in the gravy and began to eat it, and the 'Coon broke off a piece of his Johnnie cake and dipped it in the gravy and began to eat, too. And then the Crow dipped again, and the 'Possum dipped again, and the 'Coon dipped again.

"It's good," said the 'Possum.

"Yes, it's good," said the 'Coon. "Where did you get it?"

But the Crow did not tell them, and so they dipped and ate, and dipped and ate, until they dipped and ate it all up.

"Drop in again to-morrow," said the Crow when they were done.

So the next day they came again, and the next day they came again, and every day after that they came, until the storm was over and the snow was 'most gone, and Mr. Crow never did tell them the secret of it until once when he wanted to ask a great favor of Mr. 'Coon and Mr. 'Possum, but that is too long to tell about to-night.

The Story Teller looked down at the Little Lady.

She was sound asleep.

A JOKE ALL AROUND

ABOUT HOLLOW TREE PEOPLE AND THEIR WAYS

"You may tell me some more about the 'Coon and the 'Possum and the Old Black Crow," said the Little Lady, settling herself comfortably and indicating by the motion of her body that she wanted the Story Teller to rock. "They lived in three big hollow limbs of a big hollow tree, you know, and used to meet together sometimes in their parlor and talk."

Why, yes, of course. The Story Teller did know this colony, and hurriedly tried to recall some one of their many adventures. Out of the mists of that long ago time when all animals and men spoke one language and mingled more or less sociably together came presently a dim memory that cleared and brightened as it came, and took form at last in something which the Story Teller told to the Little Lady as

MR. 'COON'S BAD COLD.

THE 'COON CAUGHT A BAD COLD.

One day, early in March and during a long wet spell, the 'Coon caught a bad cold. The next morning he stayed in bed, and pulled up the covers and was cross and too sick to go out. This made extra work for the Crow and the 'Possum, who, of course, had to bring him in his meals and take care of him, and Mr. 'Coon, who found how nice it was to be waited on, thought he would take his own time about getting well. He was sick so long that by and by it set Mr. Crow to thinking, and one day, all of a sudden, he was taken ill, too, and coughed and took on, and called across to the others that he was sick and couldn't come out, either.

COUGHED AND TOOK ON.

This made still more work for the 'Possum, who now had to catch game for three, besides waiting on sick folks and taking care of their houses. So by and by Mr. 'Possum got to thinking some, as well as the others, and one morning, while the Crow and the 'Coon were lying all snug in bed and laughing to themselves at the trick they were playing, and thinking of the nice breakfast they were to have, they heard all at once the 'Possum calling out that hard work and exposure had been too much for him, and that he was sicker now than both of them put together.

Of course they had to call back to him that they were sorry, and of course they were sorry in one way, and then each of them lay down to see which would be the first to starve out.

Mr. 'Possum had a little the best of it at first, because he had brought in enough the night before to last him for a few meals, but, being very greedy, he soon ate it all up, and before long was just as hungry as either the 'Coon or the Crow, and maybe hungrier.

Every day they all grew emptier and emptier. Sometimes Mr. Crow would get up and slip to the door to see if the 'Possum or the 'Coon was not starting out for food. Sometimes Mr. 'Possum would peep out to see if the 'Coon and the Crow were not going. Sometimes Mr. 'Coon would look out to see if the Crow and the 'Possum hadn't started. Once they all saw each other, and jumped back like a flash.

GOT UP SOFTLY AND DRESSED.

That night Mr. 'Possum decided that he couldn't stand it any longer. He was so thin that his skin hung on him like a bag, and he hardly had strength enough to curl his tail. So he made a plan to slip through the parlor down stairs, and out the door at the bottom of the tree to find a good supper just for himself. A little after dark, when he thought the others were asleep, he got up softly and dressed himself and took his shoes in his hand.

LOOKING FOOLISH AND HALF STARVED.

He was afraid to put them on, for fear he would wake up the Crow and the 'Coon going down stairs.

Well, he slipped down softly, and was just about half way to the door when—biff! he ran right against something in the dark——

"But I thought you said once 'possums could see in the dark?" interrupted the Little Lady, sitting up straight.

They can in just common dark, but this, you see, was hollow tree dark, which is the very darkest dark there is. So he couldn't see a wink, and down he came and down came the other thing, too, till pretty soon—biff! they struck something else, and down all three things came over and over, rattlety-clatter, to the bottom of the stairs, right on out of the door into the moonlight, and what do you suppose was there besides Mr. 'Possum?

"I know," said the Little Lady, eagerly. "The 'Coon and the Old Black Crow?"

Exactly. Both of them dressed and looking foolish and half starved, and each with his shoes in his hand. They had all slipped down softly to get something to eat, because they were so hungry, and, of course, when they looked at each other standing there they all knew very well that none of them had been sick, except Mr. 'Coon a little right at first.

After they had looked at each other for about a minute they all began to laugh, and they laughed and laughed till they cried, and rolled on the ground and kept on laughing to think how they all had fooled each other and been fooled themselves. Then they all hurried off on a big hunt for game, and didn't get back till sunrise.

SOME NEW ACQUAINTANCES

THE LITTLE LADY IS INTRODUCED TO MR. JACK RABBIT DURING A VERY EXCITING EXPERIENCE WITH MR. DOG. THE FIRST ADVENTURE OF JACK RABBIT

HE STOPPED AND TALKED TO MR. ROBIN.

Once upon a time Mr. Jack Rabbit got up very early and set out for a morning walk. It was bright and sunny, and Mr. Rabbit was feeling so well that he walked and walked. Every little ways he stopped and talked to the Robins and Bluebirds that were up early, too, until by and by he didn't know how far away from home he really was.

"Did he know the way?" asked the Little Lady.

A LOUD BARK RIGHT BEHIND HIM.

Oh, yes, he knew the way, because you can't lose Mr. Jack Rabbit, no matter what you do, but talking along and not thinking, he had forgotten about its being so far. He was just going to turn back, though, when all of a sudden there was a great loud bark right behind him that made him jump right straight up in the air and commence running before his feet touched the ground.

He didn't stop to ask any questions. He knew that Mr. Dog was out early, too, and that he'd found his tracks and was a-coming lickety split.

"What does that mean—lickety split?"

I don't know, exactly, but Mr. Dog always runs that way when he chases Jack Rabbit, and Mr. Rabbit knew he had no time to waste.

He ran faster than Mr. Dog at first, and got far enough ahead so that when directly he saw Mr. Robin on a limb he slacked up a little minute and said:—

"Mr. Dog's coming to call, and I'm going home to get my house ready."

Then pretty soon he saw Mr. Bluebird, but he didn't have time to pause again.

"Where are you going so fast, Mr. Rabbit?" said the Bluebird.

"To get ready for Mr. Dog; he's coming to call," said the Rabbit as he went by like a streak. Then a little further on he met Mr. Turtle.

"Hi, there!" called the Turtle. "Where are you going so fast, Mr. Rabbit?"

"Dog coming—clean house!" shouted Jack Rabbit, 'most out of breath.

That made the Turtle laugh, 'cause Mr. Turtle is old and smart and he knew why the Rabbit was running so fast.

14

"Was the Rabbit so afraid of Mr. Dog?" asked the Little Lady.

He was that, but he didn't want anybody to know it if he could help it, and 'specially Mr. Dog.

Well, pretty soon Mr. Dog came by where Mr. Robin was, and he called up:—

"Hello, Mr. Robin! Has Mr. Jack Rabbit passed this way?"

"Why, yes, Mr. Dog, and he stopped a little minute to say that you were coming to see him, and that he had to hurry home to have his house ready."

That kind of surprised Mr. Dog, 'cause he thought the Rabbit was afraid of him, but he kept right on till he came to the Bluebird.

"Did Mr. Rabbit come this way?" he called up without stopping.

"Yes, sir, and hurried right on to have his house ready for you," said the Bluebird.

That surprised Mr. Dog more and more, and he began to think that after all maybe the Rabbit didn't know what he wanted of him and—

"What did he want of him?"

Well, I s'pect it was about the same as the wolf wanted of Red Riding Hood, and Jack Rabbit was so far away from home and getting so tired that there's no telling what might have happened if it hadn't been for Mr. Turtle. Mr. Turtle was a good friend to Jack Rabbit, 'cause once he beat him in a foot race by playing a trick, and he'd always felt a little sorry for it. So when Mr. Dog came along he got right in the way and said:—

"HI, THERE! HOLD ON, MR. DOG!"

"Hi, there! Hold on, Mr. Dog, or you'll get there before Mr. Rabbit is ready for you. He just passed, and said he had to clean up before you came. I s'pose he wants to get up a fine dinner, too."

Well, that settled it. Mr. Dog stopped and said he wasn't in any hurry at all, but was just running a little because it was a nice morning and he felt well. Of course, he said, he didn't want to get there before Mr. Rabbit was ready for him, and then he trotted along comfortably, thinking how he would eat the Rabbit's fine dinner first, and then there would be time enough for Mr. Rabbit himself afterward.

So, when he got to Jack Rabbit's house he straightened his vest and his necktie a little, and then he knocked and turned around and whistled while he was waiting for Mr. Rabbit to come to the door. But Jack Rabbit didn't come to the door. He opened an upstairs window and said:—

"Why, it's Mr. Dog! Sit right down on the porch, Mr. Dog, till I get my house ready and the dinner cooked."

MR. RABBIT LAUGHED AND LAUGHED.

So Mr. Dog sat down and lit his pipe and smoked and looked at the scenery, while Mr. Rabbit inside he laughed and laughed, and lay down on the bed and finally went to sleep.

Mr. Dog sat there and smoked and smoked, and wished the Rabbit would hurry and let him in, 'cause he wanted to get home to his folks, and it was a long way to travel. By and by he called up and asked him if dinner wasn't ready yet. That waked Jack Rabbit up, and he looked out the window and said that he'd had bad luck with his biscuit and dinner would be late. Then Mr. Dog said he'd come in while he was waiting, but the Rabbit said the house was full of smoke, and he wouldn't think of letting his company sit inside such a pleasant day.

Well, Mr. Dog he sat and sat, and Mr. Jack Rabbit laughed and went to sleep again, and by and by it got so late that Mr. Dog knew if he didn't go home pretty soon he'd "catch it" when he got there. So he called up again to Mr. Rabbit, and said that he'd take anything he happened to have in the house, and that he didn't care much for biscuit anyway. But Jack Rabbit said he would never show his face again if he let his company do that, and that it was a perfect shame that Mr. Dog had waited so long, when he had so far to go. He said that his stove didn't draw worth a cent, and that his fire had gone out once, and he hadn't got it started again yet.

Then Mr. Dog didn't wait to hear another word, but just set out for home, lickety split, with Mr. Jack Rabbit rolling on the bed and laughing to see him go.

"Come again, Mr. Dog!" he called after him. "Come again when you can't stay so long."

But Mr. Dog didn't say a word or look 'round, for he knew by Jack Rabbit's laughing so loud and saying to come when he couldn't stay so long that he'd been fooling him all the time.

"And did he ever go to Jack Rabbit's house again?" asked the Little Lady.

Well, not right away. He didn't go out much of anywhere after that for a while, because people made fun of him and kept calling out when he went by:—

"Come again, Mr. Dog! Come again when you can't stay so long!"

MR. RABBIT'S BIG DINNER

MR. JACK RABBIT ENTERTAINS THE HOLLOW TREE PEOPLE. AN UNWELCOME GUEST ARRIVES CAUSING SOME EXCITEMENT

THE RABBIT GETTING READY.

Once upon a time there came to the big Hollow Tree, where the 'Coon and the 'Possum and the Old Black Crow lived, an invitation from Mr. Jack Rabbit for the three to dine with him next day. Nobody was going to be there, he said, but the Turtle, and for them to come early so's to have a nice long afternoon.

17

He didn't need to say that, for the 'Possum would have started right off if it had been polite, and the Crow and the 'Coon were both so excited that the 'Coon commenced with pie first at supper and the Crow took his hat to get water in. Then they talked all the evening about their clothes and what they were going to wear, and the 'Possum said he was afraid to look at his best suit for fear it was moth eaten, and the 'Coon and the Crow rummaged through their bureaus and got out all their clean shirts so's to have one ready for the next day.

LOOKED AT THE ALBUM.

In the morning they all got up long before daylight, and the 'Possum looked out first and then called over to the others that there had been a light snow in the night, but that it was clear now and just cold enough to give a fellow a good appetite. He was going to eat a slim breakfast, he said, so's to be ready for a big dinner.

They were all dressed and ready long before time, but they managed to stand it until about ten o'clock, and then the 'Possum said he was just naturally getting gray headed waiting for that dinner, and off they started.

TROUBLE IN GETTING HIS BISCUITS TO RISE.

Mr. Jack Rabbit had got up early, too, that morning, and had the table 'most set when they came. He had his sleeves rolled up and an apron on, and the way he was flying around and getting ready was a caution. The 'Coon and the Crow sat down in the parlor, and looked at the album and some travel books they found on the table, but Mr. 'Possum was so hungry after his light breakfast that he could not keep out of the kitchen, where it smelled good, and stood around and talked to Jack Rabbit, and asked him where he got his chickens, and if he thought Mr. Fox would spare him some, too, and if Mr. Rabbit had any trouble getting his biscuits to rise in cold weather.

Then the Rabbit gave the 'Possum some new receipts, and Mr. 'Possum tasted of everything, a great big taste, making believe he wanted to see just how it was made, but really because he was almost starved, and couldn't wait.

Well, pretty soon Mr. Turtle straddled in, and everything was on the table and they all sat down. The 'Possum had tasted so much in the kitchen that he wasn't so starved as the 'Coon and the Crow, and behaved very politely, and stepped on the 'Coon's toe under the table because he ate so greedily, and whispered to the Crow not to shovel the food about on his plate, as if he were cleaning snow off a roof.

MR. JACK RABBIT FELL OVER BACKWARD.

They were all too busy to say much at first, but pretty soon they got to talking and telling stories, and Jack Rabbit told about the time that Mr. Dog chased him home, and how he kept Mr. Dog sitting out on the porch all the afternoon waiting for dinner to be ready. Then Mr. Turtle up and told about his stopping Mr. Dog that day, telling him that the Rabbit had gone home to get dinner for him, and they all laughed, and the 'Coon and the 'Possum said that Mr. Dog thought they were afraid of him, too, but the first time they got a chance they were going to show him a few things that would open his eyes. That made the Crow laugh till he coughed and strangled, and when the Rabbit said he wasn't afraid, either, the Turtle laughed, too. Then the 'Coon and the 'Possum and Mr. Jack Rabbit all pounded on the table, and said, "Just show us Mr. Dog, and you'll see whether we're afraid or not," and right then, as they said these words, there came a loud knock, and a great big bow! wow! wow! right at the door, and Mr. Jack Rabbit fell over backward, and Mr. 'Coon upset his coffee, and Mr. 'Possum, being stuffed so he could hardly move, rolled under the table and fainted dead away.

"Wasn't the Crow and Mr. Turtle scared some, too?" interrupted the Little Lady.

Not a bit. Mr. Dog is good friends with the Crow and the Turtle. Of course they were afraid some for the Rabbit and the 'Coon and the 'Possum, but they didn't think Mr. Dog could get in, because the door was locked, so they laughed and pounded on the table as the others had done and said:—

"Oh, yes, just show us Mr. Dog! Just show us Mr. Dog!"

That made the Rabbit feel ashamed, 'cause he was in his own house, so he hopped up quick and marched over to the door and said:—

"Why, Mr. Dog, is that you out there?"

Mr. Dog said it was, and that he had seen all the tracks in the snow, and just thought he'd like to take a hand in that big dinner himself. That made the hair on Mr. 'Coon's head stand right straight up, and Mr. 'Possum, who had rolled under the table, gave a groan and crawled over behind a long curtain, where he could faint and be covered up at the same time. Mr. Rabbit thought a little minute and then said, very politely:—

"It's just too bad, Mr. Dog, I'll declare it is. But every time you come it seems like something happens to keep me from having your company. We've just got up from the table and there isn't a thing left, and besides, Mr. 'Possum had a sick turn a minute ago, and we're all upside down and every which way."

But Mr. Dog said he wasn't afraid but that there'd be plenty for him to eat, and that he was a pretty good hand with sick folks himself. Then he gave another great loud bark and said:—

"You fooled me once, but you'll fool me no more,
So lift up the latch and open the door!"

Mr. Dog talks poetry that way sometimes when he gets excited. But Jack Rabbit said he really couldn't think of inviting him in, the way things were, and that it would likely be after sundown before he'd be ready for him. Of course, he said, Mr. Dog couldn't wait that long, he knew, and that he s'posed, after all, they'd have to do without his comp'ny this time. Then Mr. Dog said that his folks were away from home now, and that he could stay there all night if he wanted to, but that he didn't want to and didn't propose to, and then he gave another great big bow wow wow! and said:—

"You fooled me once, but you can't ag'in;
Open the door or I'll break it in!"

THE 'POSSUM ALMOST DIED.

Jack Rabbit and Mr. 'Coon both jumped when they heard that, and Mr. 'Possum almost died. It worried the Crow and the Turtle some, too, for they knew if he did break in the door there'd be a big row and no telling how it would end. And just then Mr. Dog gave a big run and a jump against the door, and it squeaked and opened a little, so that the Rabbit could see a streak of light through it and Mr. Dog's yellow legs and tail. When he saw that Jack Rabbit just gave one spring and landed on the top shelf of his china closet. Mr. 'Possum jumped up and ran around the room and fainted in two or three different places, trying to find one that was safer than the other, and Mr. 'Coon scampered up the Rabbit's new lace curtains and hung on to the pole for dear life. The Crow and the Turtle just kept still and got ready to argue some with Mr. Dog when he got in.

Pretty soon he came, bang! against the door again, and this time a good deal harder than before, and it squeaked louder and the crack was wider, for Mr. Dog had jumped against it as hard as ever he could, backward. And right there Mr. Dog made a mistake, for in just that little second while the crack was open the end of his tail got in it, and the door smacked right down on it, and there he was.

"Ho!" said the Little Lady. "Was he caught tight?"

He was that. The harder he pulled the tighter it pinched, and he howled like a good fellow. You wouldn't have thought that such a little bit of his tail would make him howl so loud, but it did, and he couldn't get far enough away from the door to jump against it again. Well, Mr. Rabbit didn't let on that anything had happened, but just came down out of the china closet as cool as you please, with the dessert dishes on his arm, and the 'Possum said his sick turn had passed off, and the 'Coon came down from the curtain and mentioned that he always liked to take a little exercise during a heavy meal that way. Then they had dessert, and all the time Mr. Dog was making a big fuss outside, and by and by he began to beg and promise anything if they'd just let him loose.

HE HOWLED LIKE A GOOD FELLOW.

Mr. Rabbit called out to him that, being as his folks were away now, he needn't be in any hurry, and that he might just as well stay there all night if he wanted to. Then Mr. Dog called out to the Turtle and the Crow to "prize" open the door and let him get his tail out, but they both said that they couldn't think of being impolite with Jack Rabbit in his own house by sending off any of his friends that way.

Well, pretty soon the 'Coon and the 'Possum said they must be going, they guessed, so Mr. Rabbit let them out the back door, and they went around and said goodby to Mr. Dog and hoped he was having a nice time. And Mr. Dog told them, with tears in his eyes, that he was sorry to see them go and that he hoped to meet them again. Then the 'Coon and the 'Possum both laughed and took a good look at Mr. Dog, for they had never been so close to him before in their lives. They kept on laughing and looking around as far as they could see, and said it was the best joke they had ever heard of.

THEY WALKED ALONG WITH HIM.

The Crow and the Turtle didn't go right away. They stayed and had a talk with Jack Rabbit first so as to give the 'Coon and the 'Possum time to get home. By and by they bade goodby to Mr. Rabbit and said they'd had a nice time, and went out the back door, too, and when it was shut and locked tight Jack Rabbit told Mr. Dog if he'd promise to go right home and behave himself, and not go gallivanting around the country, he'd let him loose. Mr. Dog promised, and said his tail was numb clear up to his ears, and for Mr. Rabbit to please hurry. Then Jack Rabbit got a stick of stovewood and pried the door open a little wider, and Mr. Dog's tail came out just as the Turtle and the Crow stepped around the corner.

"Was Mr. Dog mad at them?" asked the Little Lady, anxiously.

Not very. He was too much ashamed, and, besides, they walked along with him and said they were sorry and thought it was too bad the way he had been treated, and Mr. Crow said he'd have Mr. Dog over to his house for supper before long, which would be a good joke on the 'Coon and 'Possum, too, because they'd have to stay locked in their rooms. That made Mr. Dog perk up a little, but he didn't have much to say, and he didn't even look around when Mr. Jack Rabbit sat up in his window and called after them:—

"I fooled you once and I fooled you twice,
If you come again I'll fool you thrice!"

For Jack Rabbit could make up poetry, too, sometimes when he felt well.

THE CROW'S COMPANY

MR. CROW GIVES A SUPPER TO MR. DOG, ACCORDING TO PROMISE

Well, you remember (said the Story Teller) that the Crow promised Mr. Dog he would have him over sometime for supper, and play a joke on Mr. 'Coon and Mr. 'Possum. So one morning he sent word to Mr. Dog, and the same day gave it out to the 'Coon and the 'Possum that we would have company for supper the next evening, and that he was going to set the big table in the parlor and have both of them come down and take supper with him, too. He didn't tell them he was going to have Mr. Dog and went around laughing to himself, because he thought it would be very funny for them to get all ready for a fine supper and then be afraid to come down when they found out who was there. Of course he meant to tell them before they came, because he didn't really want any fuss there in the parlor, especially when he had his good things on the table.

Well, the 'Coon and the 'Possum said they'd come, and they guessed and guessed who it was that the Crow was going to have, but he wouldn't tell them, and by and by they began to suspect that maybe it was somebody that they didn't care much about. So they had a little private talk together and fixed up a way to be ready for him.

After that they went around smiling a good deal, and the Crow thought it was on account of the big supper they were expecting, so he smiled, too, and was busy getting ready for the fun next day.

Well, next day about five o'clock, Mr. Dog came and knocked at the door down stairs, and Mr. Crow slipped down and let him in, and took him right up to the parlor where supper was all on the table except the fried chicken, which he had left on the stove to keep hot. Mr. Dog took a seat and glanced round and said that everything looked good and smelled even better than it looked. The Crow liked to hear that, for he was always proud of his cooking and he laughed all over, and kept on laughing when he thought what a joke he was going to have right away on Mr. 'Coon and Mr. 'Possum.

Then, pretty soon he had everything ready, and said to Mr. Dog:—

"Now I'm going to call my friends down, but they won't come." And then they both laughed soft like, for of course Mr. Dog knew all about the joke, too.

So then the Crow went up to the 'Possum's door and knocked and said:—

"Supper's ready! Comp'ny's here! Come down!"

"WHO IS YOUR COMPANY, MR. CROW?"

"Who is your company, Mr. Crow?"

"Oh, just home folks. Nobody but Mr. Dog. We've got fried chicken and it's all ready."

"I'm sorry, Mr. Crow, but I've just had comp'ny come, too, and I couldn't come unless I brought my comp'ny."

"Who is it?" said the Crow.

"Nobody but home folks. Mr. Cat just dropped in to spend the evening."

The Old Black Crow gave a jump when he heard that, for he was afraid as death of Mr. Cat, and he said, quick as a wink:—

"Table's all full and no room for more! Table's all full and no room for more!"

Then he hurried over to the 'Coon's door and called:—

"Supper's all ready! Comp'ny's here! Come down!"

MR. 'COON PUT AN EXTRA CHAIR AGAINST THE DOOR.

Mr. 'Coon put an extra chair against the door and said:—

"Who is your comp'ny, Mr. Crow?"

"Oh, just home folks. Nobody but Mr. Dog. We've got fried chicken and it's all on the table."

"I'm sorry, Mr. Crow, but comp'ny just came here, too, and I'd have to bring him along."

"Who is it, Mr. 'Coon?"

"Only home folks. Just Mr. Hawk run in for the evening."

MR. CROW NEARLY FELL OVER BACKWARD.

Mr. Crow nearly fell over backward when he heard that. He had stolen some of Mr. Hawk's chickens the day before, and the 'Coon knew about it. The Hawk would surely know the flavor of his own chickens if he came down, and, anyhow, Mr. 'Coon would tell him. So he called out just as quick as lightning:—

"Table's all full and no room for more! Table's all full and no room for more!"

Then he hurried right back to Mr. Dog and told him not to wait, because Mr. 'Coon and Mr. 'Possum could not come, and Mr. Dog laughed and pitched into the fried chicken and said it was the best joke and the best chicken he had ever heard of. But the Crow some way did not think it was as good a joke as he had expected and could not eat his supper for looking up at the doors where the 'Possum and the 'Coon were.

By and by, when Mr. Dog had finished his supper and had a smoke, he said he guessed his folks would be looking for him and that he would have to go. Then the Crow nearly had a fit and begged and begged him to spend the evening. He said Mr. Dog came so seldom that he ought to stay, now he was there, so at last Mr. Dog sat down again and said he might as well sit a little longer, he s'posed.

28

MR. CROW TALKED AND TOLD STORIES.

Well, the Crow talked and talked and told stories and got Mr. Dog to telling stories, too, and once he slipped around behind Mr. Dog while he was talking away and put the clock back, but it didn't do any good. Mr. Dog said by and by that he was obliged to go and that he was afraid now he would be locked out when he got home. So the Crow thought as quick as he could and called out loud:—

"Time comp'ny was going home! Time comp'ny was going home!"

But the 'Possum called back that his comp'ny wasn't in any hurry. And the Coon called back that his comp'ny wasn't in any hurry either.

Then Mr. Crow was in a bad fix. He hopped around first on one foot and then on the other while Mr. Dog was putting on his things, and as soon as he was gone he skipped right up into his own room and locked the door tight.

Mr. 'Coon and Mr. 'Possum were looking out of their windows and saw Mr. Dog outside as he lit his pipe and marched off laughing. And the 'Coon and 'Possum laughed, too, for they hadn't had any company at all, but had been making believe all the time. Then they unbarred their doors and went down into the parlor, where there was a lot of the supper left, and sat down and passed the fried chicken across to each other and laughed some more and said Mr. Crow was certainly a mighty good cook.

"Didn't they give the Crow any?" asked the Little Lady, who had been so still that the Story Teller believed her asleep.

Pretty soon they did. They said it was too bad to punish him any longer, so they went up to his door, and the 'Possum knocked and said:—

"Better come down to supper, Mr. Crow. Comp'ny's all gone!"

29

And then the 'Coon he knocked and said:—

"Better come down to fried chicken, Mr. Crow. Comp'ny's all gone!"

So then the Crow opened the door a little crack and peeked out, and when he saw nobody was there but the 'Coon and the 'Possum he stepped out as brave as you please and said that he had been to one big supper and was sleepy and just going to bed, but that he believed he would sit down with them just to be sociable. He was sorry, he said, that he couldn't have asked them to bring down their comp'ny, but he hadn't fixed for so many, and, after all, it would be nicer now, all alone together.

So then the 'Coon and the 'Possum and the Old Black Crow all sat down to the table together and ate and ate and ate, and the Old Black Crow ate most of all.

THE FIRST MOON STORY

A STORY IN WHICH MR. 'COON TELLS MR. 'POSSUM AND MR. RABBIT SOMETHING ABOUT THE MOON

Last night when the full moon looked into the House of Many Windows the Little Lady stood looking at it for a long time.

She had been told that the moon was another world, and that the stars were worlds, too, and she was trying to think how that could be when they looked so small and close together; also if it were all true, and they were so big, why they did not get against each other when the sky itself wasn't any bigger than the world and came down to it everywhere at the edges. She asked the Story Teller about it when he came in.

The Story Teller tried to explain that the stars and moon were not so close together as they looked, and that some were a good deal further away than others, and a lot more things, all of which the Little Lady doubted, because she said she could see for herself that the sky was just a round blue ceiling, and that the moon and stars were right against it, and if any of them were further away than the others they would be over beyond the ceiling and wouldn't show. This was a good deal easier for the Story Teller to understand than the things he had been trying to tell, so he said, "Why, of course. I hadn't thought of that," and then he said he knew some stories about the moon that were a good deal truer, he guessed, than most anything else. And then he told her, first of all,

MR. 'COON'S STORY OF THE MOON.

Once upon a time, when Mr. Dog had invited the Crow and the Turtle to his house for supper, Jack Rabbit came over to the Hollow Tree to spend the evening with the 'Coon and the 'Possum, and they took a long walk. They walked and walked, till by and by they got to the edge of the world and sat down and hung their feet over and talked and looked at the full moon that was just rising.

They talked first about one thing and then another, and then they got to talking about the moon, and come to find out one thought it was this, and one thought it was that, and the third man, which was the 'Coon, said he knew it wasn't either one, for the moon had once belonged to his family and he knew all about it.

So then they agreed between them to let each one tell what he knew about the moon and how he came to know it and all about it. And Mr. 'Coon told first.

"Well," he said, "a long time ago, about sixteen great-great-grandfathers back, our family lived in a big woods in a big tree that was on top of a high mountain and touched the sky with its top limbs when the wind blew.

A SHINING TIN PLATE.

"It was a good big family, too; I don't know just how many there were, but I know there was an old grandmother besides the father and mother and a lot of children. They were a very noisy lot of youngsters, so the story goes, nearly all of the same age, and used to tear around the house and never want to do anything but play and run up and down stairs until my sixteenth great-great-grandmother used to stop her ears and say that those children would be the death of her, and she wished there was a school in the neighborhood so they could be sent to it.

"But those children never wanted to learn anything, and never thought about even knowing their letters, until one day Father 'Coon came home from town with a brand new shiny tin plate with the alphabet around on the edge of it. When they saw that they all made a grab for it and claimed it, but Father 'Coon held it up high and said that it was for the one that first learned his letters. He said that they were to take turns using it, a different one each time, and whoever was using it could study his letters while he was eating. He said that when it had been all around once he would see who knew the most letters and would give it to him the next time, and so on, and the first one who knew all of them should have it for his own, to keep.

BUSHY GRABBED THE PLATE.

"Well, the first night he gave it to a fellow named Bushy and sat down by him and told him the letters over and over, and all the rest leaned across the table and looked on instead of eating, all except one fellow, named Smart, who was good at learning things by heart, and he just listened and ate, too. He did that right along every meal till it came his turn, and then he pretended to look very close, but all the time he was only saying the letters over and over in his head and laughing to himself to think how he was going to surprise everybody when the time came to see who knew the most.

"And that's just what he did do. For when the plate had gone clear around and Father 'Coon called them all up one night after supper to see who could tell the most letters on it, some only knew three and some four, and some of them knew six, but when it came Smart's turn he commenced when Father 'Coon pointed to A, and said every one clear through to & just as fast as he could say them. Then the others all began to cry, and Smart took the plate and walked off with it into the next room and sat down and was saying the alphabet over and over, when all at once Bushy happened to notice that when Smart pointed out the letters for himself and said them he was just as apt to begin any place else as at A, and that he only knew them by heart and didn't know a single one when he saw it.

SHE FLUNG IT OUT THE WINDOW.

"Of course that made Bushy mad, and he ran out and told the rest that Smart didn't know his alphabet at all, and that he couldn't even tell A when it was by itself, and all the others set up a great fuss, too. They said he had to go out with the plate to Father 'Coon again, and Smart said he wouldn't do it; that it was his plate, and that he had said his letters once and didn't intend to say them again for anybody. Then Bushy grabbed the plate and said it was his, because he knew six letters, and then a little fellow named Stripe grabbed it away from Bushy because he knew six letters, too, and pretty soon they all got into a regular fight over it, and made such an awful noise that Grandmother 'Coon thought the tree was falling down, and came running in, and when she saw what they were fighting over she grabbed it away from all of them and opened the window and flung it out just as hard as ever she could fling it.

"And the tin plate went sailing and shining right straight up in the air, and kept on sailing and shining till it got to the sky; and then, of course, it couldn't get any further, but it went right on sailing and shining in the sky, and has been there, sailing and shining, ever since.

"And that," said Mr. 'Coon, "that's the moon!"

"Oh, pshaw!" said the 'Possum.

"What made those dark spots on it?" said the Rabbit.

Mr. 'Coon didn't know what to say to that just at first, and then he happened to think.

"Why," he said, "that's where they rubbed the tin off fighting over it."

"Nonsense!" said the Rabbit.

33

MR. 'POSSUM HAS SOMETHING TO SAY ABOUT THE MOON WHICH SHEDS NEW LIGHT ON THE SUBJECT

This is the story told by Mr. 'Possum when he and Mr. 'Coon and Jack Rabbit sat on the edge of the world and hung their feet over and looked at the moon:—

"Well," said Mr. 'Possum, "a good many years ago, when there were a great many more chickens than there are now, and Mr. Man took good care of them for us and let them roost in trees instead of locking them up every night in an unhealthy little pen, my folks used to go around sometimes after Mr. Man had gone to bed, and look them over and pick out what they wanted for the next day.

"I don't know why we ever began the custom of picking out our victuals at night that way, when it was dark and dangerous, but somehow we always did it, and have kept it up ever since."

"Humph!" said the 'Coon.

USED TO FALL ASLEEP AND DREAM ABOUT IT.

"Yes," continued Mr. 'Possum, "that was before there was any moon, and the nights were always dark. It wasn't a good time to choose food, and very often my folks made a mistake and got a seven-year-old bantam hen instead of a spring pullet, which is about the same size.

"This happened so much that by and by a very wise 'Possum, named Smoothe, said that if they would keep him in chickens of a youthful and tender sort he would fix up a light, so they could see and know what they were doing. They all agreed to do it, and that night Smoothe built a big fire in the top of a tall tree and sat up there and 'tended to it until nearly morning, and my folks brought home the finest lot of chickens that Mr. Man had raised for them in a good many years.

A TOP-KNOT CROW NAMED DUSK.

"Well, there was never any trouble after that to pick out young meat, and Smoothe kept the fire going nights and ate a good deal and got pretty fat, so that he didn't like to work, and kept planning some way to make his job easier. He wanted to find a light that he wouldn't have to 'tend to and keep piling wood on all night. He thought about this for a long time, and used to fall asleep and dream about it, and once he let the fire go out, and fell out of the tree and nearly gave up his job altogether.

"Well, while he was getting well he had a good deal of company, and one day a top-knot crow named Dusk came to see him. Now, you know that our friend Mr. Crow is a wise bird to-day, but in the old times a top-knot crow was wiser than anything that now flies or walks, and Dusk was a very old bird. He knew a great deal about Mr. Man and his ways, and he told Smoothe that he had seen in Mr. Man's pantry, where he went sometimes, a light that would not go out during a whole night, and that had a big bright something behind it that would throw the light in any direction. Dusk, who used to carry off almost everything he saw, whether he wanted it or not, said that he thought he might carry this light off if Smoothe would be willing to let him have a few chickens for a party he was going to give.

THE BRIGHT ROUND THING THREW THE LIGHT JUST WHERE HE WANTED IT.

"Smoothe told him he might take his pick out of his share of the chickens for the next six months if he would only bring that light, and Dusk didn't waste any time, but brought it the very next evening.

"It was a beautiful light, and Smoothe fastened it to the tip top of the tall tree, so that it would swing in any direction, and the bright round thing behind it threw the light just where he wanted it. It burned oil, and he used to fill it up with chicken oil in the evening and it would burn all night and make a better light than the fire ever did. So all he had to do was to keep it filled and turned in the direction that my folks were harvesting their chicken crop, and then he could go to bed and sleep all night if he wanted to.

"'NONSENSE!" SAID THE RABBIT.

"And that's just what he did do. And one night while he was asleep there came up a terrible storm. Of course, if Smoothe had been awake he would have taken the light down; but he wasn't awake, and the first he knew he heard broken limbs falling and crashing all around, and he jumped up and ran out just in time to see the tip top of the lamp tree break off, lamp and all, and go whirling round and round, right straight up in the air till it got to the sky, and there it stuck fast. It never went out, either, but kept on turning round and round and giving light in different directions at different times in the month.

"And that," said Mr. 'Possum, "is the moon. And you don't always see it because sometimes the bright reflecting thing is turned in the other direction. And when it's turned part way round you see part of it, and it's always been so ever since that night Smoothe went to sleep and the storm came up and carried it off."

"Humph!" said the 'Coon.

"What makes those spots on it, then?" said the Rabbit.

"Why," said Mr. 'Possum, thinking as quick as he could, "those—those are—are some leaves that blew against the reflecting thing and stayed there."

"Nonsense!" said the Rabbit.

ON THE EDGE OF THE WORLD

MR. RABBIT HAS SOMETHING TO SAY ABOUT THE MOON, DURING WHICH HE EXPLAINS THE SPOTS ON IT

This is the story that Mr. Jack Rabbit told to Mr. 'Coon and Mr. 'Possum when they sat together on the edge of the world and hung their feet over and looked at the moon. After Mr. 'Possum had finished his story, the Rabbit leaned back and swung his feet over the Big Nowhere awhile, thinking. Then he began.

"Well," he said, "my folks used to live in the moon."

"Humph!" said the 'Coon.

"Nonsense!" said the 'Possum.

"Yes," said Jack Rabbit, "they did. The moon is a world, away over on the other side of the Big Nowhere, and it doesn't stand still and stay top side up like this world, but keeps moving about and turning over, so that you have to look sharp and hang on tight to keep from falling off when it tips bottom side up, or is standing on its edge as it is to-night. My folks used to live there and Mr. Dog's folks used to live there, too. That was a long time ago, before Mr. Dog ever went to live with Mr. Man, and he was big and savage and had no more manners than he has now.

"My folks never could and never did get along with Mr. Dog's folks worth a cent, but they could mostly beat Mr. Dog's folks running, so they didn't have to associate with him unless they wanted to."

"USED TO HIDE AND WATCH FOR US."

"Of course Mr. Dog's family didn't like that, for they thought they were just as good as we were, and they used to hide and watch for us, and when we came by jump out and try to keep up with us for as much as two or three miles sometimes, just as Mr. Dog tried to keep up with me the other day, which you may remember."

The 'Possum and 'Coon grinned to themselves and nodded.

"Well," continued Mr. Rabbit, "there are some laws of etiquette—which means politeness—up there in the Moon, and they are very strict. The Old Man in the Moon makes these laws, and when one of them is broken he makes the one that breaks it just go right on doing whatever it is for nine hundred and ninety-nine years, and sometimes a good deal longer when it's a worse break than usual.

"Now the very strictest of all these laws used to be the one about Mr. Dog trying to keep up with our folks. It was called the 'Brush Pile law.' It didn't say that he couldn't keep up with us if he was able, but it did say that when we ran behind a brush pile, as we did sometimes, he must follow around the brush pile and never jump over it, no matter what happened. This was a hard law for Mr. Dog to keep, for he was mostly fat and excitable, and my folks would run around and around a brush pile, as much as a hundred times very often, and tire Mr. Dog so that he couldn't move. Then my folks would laugh and go home leisurely, while Mr. Dog would sneak off with his tongue hanging out till it dragged on the ground."

"MY TWENTY-FIRST GREAT-GREAT-GRANDFATHER COULD NOT RUN VERY FAST."

"Well, one day in the spring, when my family was out for an airing and a little sunshine, they got a good ways from home, and all of a sudden here comes Mr. Dog and his whole family, too. My folks didn't want anything to do with them, and set out for home in several directions, with Mr. Dog's folks following most all of them. My twenty-first great-great-grandfather was getting pretty old and couldn't run very fast, and there was a young, anxious looking dog named Leap quite close behind him. So the first brush pile he came to my relative paused and when Leap came around one way he went the other, and they kept that up until Leap got so mad and excited and worn out that he didn't care for the 'Brush Pile law' or anything else except my twenty-first great-great-grandfather, and all of a sudden he gave a great big bark and a high jump right straight over the top of the brush pile, and just that second the moon tipped up on its edge and all my folks and all Mr. Dog's folks came tumbling right down through the Big Nowhere to the earth, because they were all running and not holding on—all except Leap, who stayed right up in the air, according to law, and he has been there ever since.

"IT'S JUST AS PLAIN AS CAN BE."

"And when my folks and Mr. Dog's folks got down to the earth they were all so scared that my folks ran in one direction and Mr. Dog's folks ran in another. The dog family kept on running till they got to Mr. Man's house, and there they hid and stayed."

"And since that day," concluded Mr. Jack Rabbit, "there has never been any of our family in the moon, and Leap is the only dog there. He's still jumping over the brush pile because he broke the law, and you can see him there any clear night when the moon sits up on its edge as it does now. And that's what those spots are—a dog jumping over a brush pile. It's just as plain as can be."

The 'Possum and the 'Coon looked up at the full moon and said that the spots certainly did look a good deal like Mr. Dog jumping over a brush pile, but that the Rabbit couldn't prove his story any more than they could prove theirs, and that it wasn't any better story, if it was as good.

"Of course I can prove it," said the Rabbit. "There is an old adage about it, and you can prove anything by an old adage. It goes this way:—

"The longest way is often best—
Never jump over a cuckoo's nest.

"I don't know just why it says 'cuckoo's nest,' but I suppose cuckoos always used to build in brush piles in the moon, and maybe they do yet. Anyhow it proves it."

"Why, yes," said the 'Coon. "Sure enough!"

"That's so! It does!" said the 'Possum.

40

MR. CROW SPENDS A SOCIAL EVENING WITH MR. DOG

Once upon a time, said the Story Teller, when the Old Black Crow was visiting Mr. Dog——

"Was that the night that Mr. Rabbit and the rest told their moon stories?" interrupted the Little Lady.

The very same night, and the Crow and Mr. Dog got to telling stories, too.

They told pig stories because they both knew a good deal about pigs, and Mr. Dog, being in his own house, let the Crow tell first. Mr. Crow said he was going to tell a true story, so he lit his pipe and began this way:—

MR. CROW'S STORY OF THE LITTLE PIG.

Well, said Mr. Crow, there was once a lot of little pigs that lived in a large pen with the big mother pig and were very fat and happy—all but one.

This poor little fellow was what is called a runt pig, because he was not nearly so big as the others, nor so strong. They crowded him away at dinner time, so that he barely got enough to live on, and stayed small and thin, while the others grew every day fatter and fatter.

At last the little runt pig made up his mind that he would run away and be a wild pig such as he had heard his brothers and sisters talk about sometimes after supper.

He thought about it a good deal, and one morning bright and early he started. Being so little, he squeezed through a small hole in the back of the pen, and then ran away very fast, without stopping to look behind. He ran and ran, straight across the barnyard, where there were some chickens scratching, and out into a big field. When he got so tired that he could go no further he stopped for a little, and then ran on again.

"OH, HERE'S THE WOODS!"

He had to go a long way, but by and by he saw a lot of trees, and said, "Oh, here's the woods! Now I'll be a wild pig!" So he squeezed between two boards that made a crack in the fence, and under the trees he saw a lot of ripe peaches and apples, for he was in a big orchard.

It was just peach time, and the little pig was very hungry.

HE BEGAN SQUEALING FOR HIS MOTHER.

So he ate and ate, first a lot of peaches, and then a lot of apples; then a lot more peaches, and then a good many more apples. Then he picked out only the ripest and finest apples and peaches as he came to them, and ate and kept on eating until he had pains in his stomach and began squealing for his mother.

"Oh, oh, oh!" he squealed. "I am going right home!" But when he came to the fence he had eaten so much fruit that he could not get through the crack again and stuck fast half way. Then he squealed louder than ever, and pretty soon somebody said:—

"Why, here's a little pig fast in the fence!" And Mr. Man came through the orchard and took hold of the little pig's hind legs and pressed the boards apart so's not to hurt him.

"Whose pig are you, I want to know?" he said as he pulled him out.

Then Mr. Man took the little pig under his arm and went back through the orchard with him to his house.

"Here's a little runt pig I found stuck fast in our fence," he said to Mrs. Man when he got there. "He's eaten too many apples and peaches, I should think, by the way he looks and squeals."

Then he fixed up a nice box for him, with clean straw in it, and gave him some warm milk in a pan. By and by the little pig went to sleep.

Every day Mr. Man and his wife brought him nice things to eat, and soon the little pig grew so fat that they had to put him in a larger pen. Then they fed him still more, and, being all alone, he ate just as much as he wanted. So he grew and grew, fatter and fatter, and every few weeks they had to put him in a larger pen, until people came from all over the country to see what a beautiful large pig he was. Then by and by there was a fair where all the fine pigs were taken for show, and Mr. Man and Mrs. Man and the little runt pig all went to the fair, but the little pig wasn't a little runt pig any more, for he took the first prize for being the largest and finest pig at the fair.

HE TOOK THE FIRST PRIZE.

THE SECOND PIG STORY

MR. DOG TELLS OF ANOTHER RUNAWAY WHO HAS A STRANGE ADVENTURE

When Mr. Crow had finished the story about the little runt pig Mr. Dog nodded and said that was a good story and that he knew the mate to it. So then he filled up his pipe, too, and lit it and leaned back and told the story about

43

AS BIG AS YOU PLEASE.

"This," said Mr. Dog, "is the story of a saucy pig—a saucy, fat pig, with a curly tail. He wasn't good to his brothers and sisters, and was greedy, and not very clean, either, because he wouldn't wear his bib at the table, and often grabbed things and tipped them over, instead of being polite and taking what his mother put on his plate.

"Besides this, the saucy pig, who was called Curly, used to boast of how strong he was, and how fast he could run and how far he could jump, and when he heard some story about a little runt pig who ran away and made his fortune—the same one you told, perhaps—he went around boasting that he could do that any day, and that he could run twice as far as any little runt pig, and get twice as fat and take twice as big a prize at the fair."

44

HE COULDN'T GET THROUGH.

"Well, he talked and bragged about it so much that by and by he really believed he could do everything he said, and made up his mind to run away sure enough. He didn't creep out through a hole and slip away, as your little pig did, but took a pretty valise that he had got for Christmas and put all his things in it, and some of his brothers' and sisters' things, too, and then put on his best suit and walked out the front door, as big as you please, with the others all looking at him and wishing they were as big and strong as Curly, so they could go, too, or take their playthings away from him, they didn't care which. Then one of them ran back and said, 'Oh, ma, Curly's running away! Curly's running away, ma, and he's taken our things!'

"But Curly's mother didn't worry much. 'Oh, well, just let him go,' she said. 'He'll be back quick enough.' Then she took her afternoon nap, and Curly walked out across the meadow, sniffing the sunshine and talking to himself about what he was going to do.

"Then he remembered that the little runt pig had run, and Curly thought he ought to run some, too, but he was so fat he couldn't run far, and had to sit down to rest, and then he walked on again and kept walking until he thought he must be almost to the edge of the world, which his mother had told him was just beyond the woods. He was getting very tired, when all at once he came to a gate and looked up, and there was an orchard full of ripe apples and peaches, just as the little runt pig had found. The cracks in the fence were too small for him to try to get through, but he thought he could wiggle under the gate. So he got down in the dust with his new clothes and wiggled and wriggled, but he couldn't get through, and when he tried he couldn't get back, either.

45

RAN TO HIS MOTHER.

"Then he began to squeal. He could squeal louder than any two other pigs almost, and by and by Mr. Man, who was working in the next field, heard him and came running. When Curly heard Mr. Man coming he thought, 'Now he'll take me home and make me a great pig, just as he did the little runt pig.' But Mr. Man didn't. 'Here, you rascal!' he said, what are you doing under my gate? I'll fix you.' Then he picked up a long, scratchy stick and commenced to beat Mr. Curly, first on one side and then on the other, till he squealed and howled so loud that you could hear him almost a mile. Then Mr. Man caught him by the leg and opened the gate and pulled him out. 'Now, you go home!' he said, and Curly started, but he was so frightened that he didn't know where home or any place else was, and he scampered off without his hat or playthings, and ran and ran and ran till he almost dropped. And just then one of my family, who had been digging out a mole, happened to see the pig running and took after him and caught him and dragged him round and round by the ear till Mr. Man came running and parted them and held my relative by the collar while he pushed Curly with his foot in the other direction.

"'Now I guess you'll go home!' he said, and Curly thought so, too, and limped off, trying to run. It was such a long way back home that it seemed as if he never would get there. Every minute he thought he heard my cousin coming after him, but he couldn't run any more to save his life, and his ear was bleeding and hurt him, and he cried and squealed, and when at last he did get home he slipped in the back way and tried to wash his face and brush his clothes before they saw him, but they all saw him come in, with his sore ear and his nice, new clothes all torn and dirty. Then they began to laugh and point at him, and said:—"

"'Oh, here comes Curly, the runaway. He's been to the fair and brought home the red ribbon on his ear!' And that was the very meanest thing they could say, for, of course, they meant the red blood on his ear, and poor Curly ran to his mother and cried and sobbed as if his heart would break and said he would never, never run away again as long as he lived.

"And I've heard," concluded Mr. Dog, "that he never did."

MR. DOG TAKES LESSONS IN DANCING

JACK RABBIT PLAYS ONE MORE JOKE ON MR. DOG

MR. RABBIT WAS MAKING SOAP
IN THE BACK YARD.

After Mr. Dog had finished his pig story he and Mr. Crow got to talking over old times and telling what happened to them when they were boys and how everything had changed and how young fellows now had things pretty much their own way and no trouble to get an education.

Mr. Crow said that he believed if he'd had half a chance when he was young he'd have made an artist. He said he used to draw off likenesses on his slate so that anybody could almost tell who they were and that the 'Coon and the 'Possum each had in their rooms in the Big Hollow Tree pictures of themselves that he had drawn which were just as good to-day as the day they were made.

Mr. Dog thought it was mighty fine to be talented like that. He said that his early education had been neglected, too, and that he knew he might have been a poet, for he could make rhymes just as easy as falling off a log, and that he knew three rhymes for every word he could think of except "silver" and "orange." Of course, it was too late now, and he had mostly given up poetry and thought some of going into society. All he needed was good clothes and a few instructions in manners and some dancing lessons. He said he was just as young and just as good looking as he ever was, and that in a few days he'd have some new clothes. Then he asked Mr. Crow if he knew of anybody that would give him some lessons in politeness and dancing.

Mr. Crow thought a while, and then said that he didn't know of a soul in the neighborhood that could be so polite and dance as well as Mr. Jack Rabbit, and that he didn't suppose Mr. Rabbit and Mr. Dog were on good terms. That made Mr. Dog feel pretty bad, 'cause he knew it was just that way, and by and by he got Mr. Crow to promise that he would go and call on Jack Rabbit next morning and see if he couldn't fix it up somehow for him to take a few lessons. So next morning Mr. Crow called over to see Mr. Rabbit, and found him making

47

soap out in the back yard. He had a good fire built between some stones and a big kettle full of brown stuff, which he was stirring with a long stick. He seemed to be feeling pretty well, for he kept singing,

"Fire and stir, and grease and lye—
Soap to scrub with by and by."

"Ho!" said the Little Lady. "Do they make soap like that?"

They used to in old times. They made what they called a lye by running water through new wood ashes, and then they put grease in it and boiled it in a big kettle. It was very strong soap, and people didn't wash their hands with it, because it got into sore places and burnt and stung like fury. But they used it a good deal to scrub with, and Jack Rabbit made it himself because he was smart and knew how.

BOWED POLITELY, AS IF HE WERE MEETING LADIES.

Well, the Crow told him all about what Mr. Dog had said, and Mr. Rabbit kept stirring and singing kind of soft like to himself, and smiling a little, and by and by, when the Crow was done, he said that of course Mr. Dog wasn't very polite, and that some lessons would certainly do him good. As for dancing, he said that if Mr. Dog would promise to do just as he told him he would be able to dance as many as three different steps in less than five minutes after he got there.

Mr. Crow said that Mr. Dog had promised anything, and that he would send him over that very afternoon. And, sure enough right after dinner, here comes Mr. Dog, lickety split, to take lessons. Jack Rabbit had his door locked and his window open, and was sitting by it and looking out when Mr. Dog got there. He told Mr. Dog to sit right down and catch his breath a little, and then the lessons would begin. His kettle of soap was all done, and he had taken it off of the fire, but the fire wasn't out yet, though it looked as if it was, because it had burned down to coals and white ashes.

48

Mr. Rabbit had his new soap in the house, and he spread some of it on a cloth and tossed it down to Mr. Dog.

GAVE A HOWL AND JUMPED STRAIGHT UP INTO THE AIR.

"That's a dance plaster," he said, "but you don't put it on quite yet. The first thing will be some lessons in politeness. You must look straight at me and do just as I tell you."

Mr. Dog said that he would do that, and took a seat facing Mr. Rabbit and paid close attention. Then Jack Rabbit got up and bowed politely, as if he were meeting ladies, and, of course, took a step or two backward as he bowed, and then Mr. Dog bowed and took some steps backward, too. And then he sat down, and Mr. Rabbit told him just where his mistakes were, and made him do it over and over until Mr. Dog had bowed and scraped and backed himself almost into the fire, though he didn't know it.

Next, Jack Rabbit said, they'd have a lesson in paying compliments, and then the dancing. Now, whenever anybody pays a compliment to Mr. Dog he always wags his tail; so the Rabbit thought of the very finest compliment he could think of and paid it to Mr. Dog, and Mr. Dog forgot that it was only a lesson and was so happy to receive such a compliment from Mr. Jack Rabbit that he wagged his tail a great big wag sideways and then up and down, until all at once he gave a howl and jumped straight up in the air, for he had pounded his tail right into the ashes and hot coals of Mr. Rabbit's fire.

TOOK OVER THE HILL
TOWARDS HOME.

"Did it burn him much?" asked the Little Lady.

It did that, and he howled and jumped up and down and whirled first one way and then the other, and Jack Rabbit leaned out of the window and held his sides and said:—

"That's it! That's the step! Dance, Mr. Dog; dance!"

When Mr. Dog heard that, he thought the Rabbit was really in earnest, and didn't know, perhaps, he had wagged his tail into the fire; so he quit howling and really tried to do a few fancy steps, and Jack Rabbit almost died trying to keep from laughing, but he managed to do it, and he called out to Mr. Dog that he was doing fine, and that all he needed now was the dance plaster on his tail. When Mr. Dog heard that, he thought perhaps a dance plaster would take the smart away, too, and he sat right down and tied it on, tight. And then pretty soon that soft soap began to act, and, right then, of all the howling and dancing and performance that you ever heard of, Mr. Dog did it. Mr. Rabbit couldn't hold in any longer, and lay back in his chair, and laughed, and rolled on his bed and shouted, and when Mr. Dog heard him he knew he had been fooled again, and he took off over the hill toward home a good deal faster than he came. Every little ways he'd stop to dance and perform, and try to get that plaster off his tail, and every time he stopped Jack Rabbit would sing out:—

"That's a new step, Mr. Dog! You're doing fine! Dance, Mr. Dog; dance!"

And for a long time after that Mr. Dog didn't like to go out much, because everywhere he went somebody would be sure to say to him:—

"That's a new step, Mr. Dog! Dance, Mr. Dog; dance!"

MR. RABBIT'S UNWELCOME COMPANY

MR. POLECAT MAKES A MORNING CALL AND MR. DOG DROPS IN

"I think I shall have to tell you about Mr. Polecat," said the Story Teller, "and about his visit to Mr. Rabbit."

"Who's Mr. Polecat?" said the Little Lady. "You never told me about him before."

"Well, no, because you see Mr. Polecat is so queer in some of his ways that people even don't talk about him a great deal. He is really quite a nice gentleman, though, when he doesn't get excited. But when he does he loses friends.

"The trouble is with the sort of perfumery he uses when he gets excited, just as some people use a smelling bottle, and nobody seems to like the sort Mr. Polecat uses except himself. I suppose he must like it or he wouldn't be so free with it. But other people go away when he uses it—mostly in the direction the wind's blowing from—and in a hurry, as if they were afraid they'd miss a train. Even Mr. Dog doesn't stop to argue with Mr. Polecat. Nobody does, and all the other deep woods people do their best to make him happy and to keep him in a good humor whenever he comes about, and give him their nicest things to eat and a lot to carry home with him, so he'll start just as soon as possible.

"But more than anything they try to keep him from saying anything about Mr. Dog or hinting or even thinking about Mr. Dog, for when he does any of these things he's apt to get excited, and then sometimes he opens up that perfume of his and his friends fall over each other to get out of reach. They're never very happy to see him coming, and they're always glad to see him go, even when he's had a quiet visit and goes pretty soon, which is just what didn't happen one time when he came to call on Jack Rabbit, and it's that time I'm going to tell about.

"Mr. Rabbit looked out his door one morning and there was Mr. Polecat, all dressed up, coming to see him. He wasn't very far off, either, and Mr. Rabbit hardly had time to jerk down a crayon picture of Mr. Dog that he'd made the day before, just for practice. He pushed it under the bed quick, and when Mr. Polecat came up he bowed and smiled, and said what a nice day it was, and that he'd bring a chair outside if Mr. Polecat would like to sit there instead of coming in where it wasn't so pleasant.

"But Mr. Polecat said he guessed he'd come in, as it was a little chilly and he didn't feel very well anyway. So he came inside, and Jack Rabbit gave him his best chair and brought out a little table and put a lot of nice things on it that Mr. Polecat likes, and began right away to pack a basket for him to take home.

"But Mr. Polecat didn't seem to be in any hurry to go. He ate some of the nice things, and then leaned back to talk and smoke, and told Mr. Rabbit all the news he'd heard as he came along, and Mr. Rabbit got more and more worried, for he knew that just as likely as not Mr. Polecat had heard something about Mr. Dog and would begin to tell it pretty soon, and then no knowing what would happen. So Jack Rabbit just said 'Yes' and 'No' and began to talk about Mr. Robin, because Mr. Robin was a good friend of everybody and nobody could get excited just talking about Mr. Robin. But Mr. Polecat says:—'Oh, yes, I saw Mr. Robin as I came along, and he called to me that Mr. Dog——' And then Jack Rabbit changed the subject as quick as he could and spoke about Mr. Squirrel, and Mr. Polecat says:—'Oh, did you hear how Mr. Squirrel went over to Mr. Man's house and saw Mr. Dog there——' And then poor Mr. Rabbit had to think quick and change the subject again to the Hollow Tree people, and Mr. Polecat said:—'Oh, yes. I stopped by that way as I came along, and they called out to me from up stairs how you were practising drawing, and that you gave Mr. Dog some dancing lessons the other day, and then made a fine picture of him just as he looked when he danced into the hot coals, so I hurried right over here for just to see that picture.'

"Poor Mr. Rabbit! He didn't know what to do. He knew right away that the Hollow Tree people had told about the picture to get rid of Mr. Polecat, and he made up his mind that he'd get even with them some day for getting him in such a fix. But some day was a long ways off and Mr. Polecat was right there under his nose, so Mr. Rabbit said, just as quick as he could say it, that the Hollow Tree people were always making jokes, and that the picture was just as poor as it could be, and that he'd be ashamed to show it to anybody, much more to a talented gentleman like Mr. Polecat. But that made Mr. Polecat all the more anxious to see it, for he was sure Mr. Rabbit was only modest, and pretty soon he happened to spy the edge of the picture frame under Mr. Rabbit's bed, and just reached under and pulled it out, before Mr. Rabbit could help himself.

"Well, he picked up that picture and looked at it a minute, and Jack Rabbit began to back off toward the door and say a few soothing words, when all at once Mr. Polecat leaned back and commenced to laugh and laugh at the funny picture Mr. Dog made where Mr. Rabbit called to him, 'Dance! Mr. Dog, dance!' And then, of course, Mr. Rabbit felt better, for if his company thought it was funny and laughed there wasn't so much danger.

"'Why,' said Mr. Polecat, 'it's the best thing I ever saw! You could almost imagine that Mr. Dog himself was right here, howling and barking and dancing.'

"'Oh, no, hardly that,' said Mr. Rabbit. 'Of course I suppose it is a little like him, but it's not at all as if he were here, you know—not at all—and he's ever so far off, I'm sure, and won't come again for a long time. You know, he's——'

"'Oh, yes, it is!' declared Mr. Polecat. 'It's just as if he were right here. And I can just hear him howl and bark, and——'

"And right there Mr. Polecat stopped and Mr. Rabbit stopped, and both of them held their breath and listened, for sure enough they did hear Mr. Dog howling and barking and coming toward the house as straight as he could come.

"Jack Rabbit gave a jump right up in the air, and hollered, 'Run! Mr. Polecat, run! and go the back way!' But Mr. Polecat never runs from anybody—he doesn't have to—he just opens up that perfume of his and the other people do the running. So Mr. Rabbit gave one more jump, and this time he jumped straight up the chimney, and didn't stop till he got to the roof, where he found a loose board and put it over the chimney quick and sat down on it. Then he called to Mr. Dog, who was coming lickety-split through the woods:—

"'Why, how are you, Mr. Dog? Glad to see you! Walk right in. There's company down stairs; just make yourself at home till I come down.' You see there was no use to stop him now, because Mr. Rabbit could tell by what was coming up the chimney that it was too late, and he wanted Mr. Dog to get a good dose of it as well as himself.

"And Mr. Dog did come just as hard as he could tear, for the wind was blowing toward the house and he couldn't detect anything wrong until he gave a great big jump into Mr. Rabbit's sitting room and right into the midst of the most awful smell that was ever turned loose in the Big Deep Woods.

"Well, it took Mr. Dog so suddenly that he almost fainted away. Then he gave a howl, as if a wagon had run over his tail, and tumbled out of that sitting room and set out for home without once stopping to look behind him. Then Mr. Rabbit laughed and laughed, and called:—

"'Come back! Mr. Dog. Came back and stay with us. Mr. Polecat's going to spend a week with me. Come back and have a good time.'

"But Mr. Dog didn't stop, and he didn't seem to hear, and by and by Mr. Polecat called up that he was going home and that Mr. Rabbit could come down now, for Mr. Dog was gone and wouldn't come back, he guessed. But Mr. Rabbit said no, he didn't feel very well yet and guessed he'd stay where he was for the present, and that if Mr. Polecat was going he might leave both doors open and let the wind draw through the house, because he always liked to air his house after Mr. Dog had been to see him. Then Mr. Polecat took his basket and went, and Jack Rabbit didn't come down for a long time, and when he did he couldn't stay in his house for the awful smell. So he went over to stay a week with the Hollow Tree people, and his clothes didn't smell nice, either, but they had to stand it, and Mr. Rabbit said it served them right for getting him into such a fix. It was over a week before he could go back to his house again, and even then it wasn't just as he wanted it to be, and he aired it every day for a long time.

"But there was one thing that made him laugh, and that was when he heard from Mr. Robin how Mr. Dog got home and Mr. Man wouldn't have him about the house or even in the yard, but made him stay out in the woods for as much as ten days, until he had got rid of every bit of Mr. Polecat's nice perfumery."

HOW MR. DOG GOT EVEN

THE FOREST FRIENDS PREPARE FOR A MAY PARTY AND ARRANGE FOR A QUIET TIME

Well, yes, said the Story Teller, Mr. Dog did have a good deal of trouble, and it makes me sorry for him sometimes when I think about it. He still kept good friends with the Crow and the Turtle, though, and was on pretty fair terms with Mr. Robin and most all the rest of the Bird family, besides living in the same yard with Mr. Man, who always kept an eye on him and got him out of trouble when he could. Of course Jack Rabbit and the Hollow Tree people mostly got the best of Mr. Dog, but there was one time when they didn't. This is how it happened.

Once upon a time Mr. Jack Rabbit was spending the evening over at the big Hollow Tree with the Crow and the 'Coon and the 'Possum. They had all had their supper, and were leaning back and talking about the weather and what a late spring it had been, and how bad the cold rains were for young chickens. Mr. Rabbit didn't care for chickens himself, but he usually kept some for his friends, and always had a nice patch of young clover and some garden vegetables for his own use. He said the late frost had killed his early lettuce and young cabbage plants, and that his clover patch looked as if a fire had been through it.

Mr. 'Coon smoked a little and looked into the fire and said that he guessed to-morrow would be a warm day, and the Crow said he knew it would be because he could feel it in his leg, where a stray shot from Mr. Man's gun happened to hit him once when he was taking a walk in Mr. Man's cornfield just about this time of year.

The 'Possum put his thumbs in the armholes of his vest and leaned back against the mantel, and said he had a plan he wanted to tell them about. When he said that they all kept still to listen, because they knew when the 'Possum had a plan it always meant something good to eat, and they were always ready to hear about good things to eat, even when they'd just got up from the supper table.

Mr. 'Possum puffed a few puffs of smoke, and then he went on to say that after so much bad weather in April he thought it would be proper for them to give an outdoor feast and a woods party on the first day of May. All the others spoke up right off and said that was just the thing. Then they all began talking at once about what each would bring and whom they should invite.

HE FELT FOR THE INVITATION.

Jack Rabbit said he would invite Mr. Chipmunk and Mr Quail, and that he would speak a piece composed for the occasion. The 'Coon said he would invite Mr. Fox, because he had the best chickens, and would bring a basket of them along. The 'Possum said that would be a good plan, and that they ought to try as much as they could to invite people that would bring things. That made the Crow laugh, and he said if they wanted to do that they might invite Mr. Man himself.

FORGOT HE'D EVER HAD ANY TROUBLE IN HIS LIFE.

Of course all the others laughed at first when they heard that, and then, all at once, they quit laughing, for speaking of Mr. Man made them think of Mr. Dog, and they knew how he was always trapesing around the country where he wasn't wanted, and just as likely as not would walk right in on them at dinner time and make it unpleasant for everybody.

They all felt pretty lonesome when they thought of that, and then the Crow laughed again and said he would send over a note by Mr. Robin to Mr. Dog inviting him to go and see some friends of his that had just moved across the Wide Grass Lands. He said Mr. Dog would be glad to go, and that his friends would be glad to see him, and that it would take all day to make the trip and do no harm to anybody. Then all of them felt well again.

Mr. Crow wrote the note right away, and when he invited the Robin to the May party next morning he asked him if he would take Mr. Dog's invitation over to him and slip it under his door before he was up. He said it was to be a surprise for Mr. Dog, and he didn't want him to know just who sent the invitation. He didn't tell the Robin that it was an invitation for Mr. Dog to get out of the country, because the Robin is a good bird and wouldn't help to deceive anybody for the world.

54

AT MR. FOX'S HOUSE THE FEATHERS WERE FLYING.

Mr. Robin was tickled 'most to death at his own invitation, and slipped Mr. Dog's in his pocket, and hurried off with it just as fast as ever he could. He was so excited that he forgot he had a hole in the pocket of his coat, and never thought of it till he got to Mr. Man's yard, where Mr. Dog's house was. Then he remembered all at once, and when he felt for the invitation and turned his pocket inside out there was the hole all right, but the invitation was gone.

TOOK ONE MORE LOOK AT HIMSELF IN THE GLASS.

Mr. Robin at first didn't know what to do. Then he happened to think that all Mr. Crow had said was that he didn't want Mr. Dog to know just who sent it to him, so he went right up to Mr. Dog's house and rapped. Mr. Dog came out yawning, but when he heard that he was invited to a May party he forgot that he'd ever had any trouble in his life, and danced and rolled over and wagged his tail, till the Robin thought he was having a fit. Then when Mr. Dog heard that the party was gotten up mostly on his own account, and was to be a kind of a surprise, he had another fit, and said he never was so happy in the world. Mr. Robin said he couldn't tell him just who sent the invitation, but he told him a few of those invited, and Mr. Dog grew six inches taller and said he must certainly have some more new clothes for a party like that.

Then Mr. Robin set off home to get ready, for there were only two days more in April and everybody had to scramble around to be ready in time, especially Mr. Jack Rabbit, who had to write a poem. Over at Mr. Fox's house the feathers were flying, and at the Hollow Tree Mr. Crow had his sleeves rolled up, baking all day long. The 'Coon sat in his room and rocked and planned games, and the 'Possum followed Mr. Crow about and told him new things to cook. Everywhere in the woods, and even out in the Wide Grass Lands, folks were staying up nights to get ready, but none of them felt as happy or took as much trouble to look well as Mr. Dog. He knew there couldn't be any joke this time, because Mr. Robin had invited him, and Mr. Robin wouldn't play a joke on anybody. Every little while he would go out and roll on the grass in the sun and then go in and put on his new clothes and stand before the glass. Then he would march up and down and try to see if his coat wrinkled under the arms and if his trousers fitted neatly around the waist. As he thought the party was to be given for him, of course he wasn't expected to bring anything except all the style he could put on, and when the morning came Mr. Dog did put on all he could carry, and took one more look at himself in the glass and started. He had never felt so happy in his life.

HOW MR. DOG GOT EVEN

CONTINUED
THE SURPRISE OF MR. RABBIT AND OTHERS

Poor Mr. Dog! He did not dream that the Robin had made a big mistake when he invited him. He was all ready for a grand time and thought he was to be the guest of honor. But the 'Coon and the 'Possum and all the rest thought he was in another part of the country that day, and when they got to the place where the party was to be they shook hands and laughed about how Mr. Crow had played it on Mr. Dog and then rolled on the grass and cut up in a great way.

Mr. Fox was there with all his folks, and Mr. Squirrel and his folks, and Mr. Weasel and Mr. Woodchuck and Mrs. Quail, and ever so many others. Mr. Rabbit had picked out the spot, which was a pretty, green, open place in the woods, and right in the centre of it a little weeping willow tree, with long, trailing branches like ribbons. This was to be their May pole, and they were so happy that they commenced dancing almost as soon as they got there. Mr. Dog, of course, hadn't arrived yet. It had taken him so long to dress, and then he had a long way to come, so he was late.

Pretty soon Mr. 'Possum puffed and blowed because he was so fat, and said he thought they ought to sit right down and begin to eat, and let Mr. Jack Rabbit read his poem to them through the first course. The Rabbit was willing to do that, for he would rather read his own poetry than eat any time, and, besides, the first course was something he didn't like very well. So then they all sat down around the table cloth which they had spread on the grass, and Mr. Rabbit got up and put his right hand in the breast of his coat. He commenced by saying that his friends seemed to think he was a good deal of a poet, but that he had always been too busy to really write his best, and that all his poems, like the one he was just about to read, had been little inspirations tossed off on the spur of the moment. Of course, everybody there knew that Jack Rabbit had sat up two whole days and nights to write his poem, but they all cheered and clapped their hands, and Mr. Rabbit bowed and coughed a little and began to read:—

WHEN MR. DOG'S AWAY.

By J. Rabbit.

Oh, 'tis happy in the woodland
When Mr. Dog's away;
'Tis happy in the woodland
Upon the first of May.
He's gone across the grassland
We hope he's gone to stay;
Then don't forget the feast is set
And Mr. Dog's away.

The Robin was just about to speak up at this moment and say that Mr. Dog was surely coming, but the others cheered so that nobody heard him, and Mr. Rabbit went on with his poem.

Then 'tis hey! for Mr. Woodchuck!
And tis hi! for Mrs. Quail!
And 'tis ho! for Mr. 'Possum
With a bowknot on his tail!
Then 'tis hip! for Mr. Robin
And for all the rest, hurray!
The friends are met, the feast is set,
And Mr. Dog's away.

"Hurray! hurray!" shouted all the others. "The friends are met, the feast is set, and Mr. Dog's away!"

Then hand around the glasses
And fill them to the brim,
And drink a health to Mr. Dog,
For we are fond of him.
And, though he be not present
Upon this happy day,
We'll fill the cup and drink it up
To Mr. Dog away!

SAW THAT SOMETHING WAS WRONG.

At the last line everybody was just about to lift their glasses and give a great big cheer for the poem, when all at once they saw by Jack Rabbit's face that something was wrong. Then they all looked where he was looking, and there, right before them, bowing and smiling, stood Mr. Dog himself! He had just come in time to hear the last stanza of the poem and was ready to dance with joy, he was so happy to think they were drinking his health when he wasn't there.

He felt so good that he didn't notice how surprised they looked, and slipped into a seat at the table, saying he was sorry to be late, and that he had just heard the last lines of Mr. Rabbit's poem, but that they had made him very proud and happy, and he hoped Mr. Jack Rabbit would read it again for his benefit.

Of course, nearly everybody there was scared almost into fits, but they didn't dare to let on, for they saw that there had been an awful mistake somewhere, and if Mr. Dog found it out and knew he hadn't been invited no telling what might happen. Jack Rabbit smiled, kind of sickly like, and said that he had been overcome by the excitement, and didn't feel quite able to read the poem again. He said he hoped Mr. Dog would judge the first verses, though, by the last, and feel just as glad to be there as they were to have him. And all the rest said, "Oh, yes, so glad to have Mr. Dog with us," and kept piling things oh his plate, so he wouldn't want anything to eat besides his dinner. Mr. Dog felt so well and was in such a good humor that he commenced pretty soon to tell stories and jokes on himself, and by and by told about the time he went over to take dancing lessons of Jack Rabbit.

HE SET OUT FOR HOME.

Everybody thought at first that they'd better laugh at Mr. Dog's jokes, and they did laugh like everything, but when he started that story about what Mr. Rabbit had done to him they didn't know whether to laugh or not. Some laughed a little and some didn't, and Mr. Rabbit said he thought it was getting a little too warm for him there in the sun, and he believed he'd go and sit in the shade a minute and cool off, so he went over behind some waxberry bushes, where it was shady, and the minute he got where Mr. Dog couldn't see him he set out for home just about as fast as he could travel, without stopping to say goodby or to look behind him.

MR. DOG MADE A SPEECH.

Pretty soon Mr. 'Coon said he thought mebbe Mr. Rabbit was sicker than he let on, and he guessed he'd better go and see about it. So he went over behind the waxberry bushes, too, and was half way home before you could say "Jack Robinson." Then Mr. 'Possum told Mr. Crow that he hoped he and the others would entertain Mr. Dog a while, for he knew Mr. 'Coon would need help, and away he went, and before long Mr. Fox and Mr. Woodchuck, and Mr. Squirrel and all their folks had gone over behind the waxberry bushes to look after Mr. Rabbit too, and none of them wasted a minute's time making tracks for home as soon as they got out of sight.

THE THREE FRIENDS.

But the Crow and the Turtle and the Robin didn't go because they were all on good terms with Mr. Dog. Mrs. Quail didn't go either, though before long most everybody else had gone. Then Mr. Crow said he guessed poor Mr. Rabbit's friends had taken him home, and Mr. Dog said he was sorry, and that it was too bad anything should happen that way when folks were having such a good time. He said he'd call at Jack Rabbit's house next day to see how he was and hear the rest of that poem. Then Mr. Crow and Mr. Turtle laughed and laughed, and Mr. Dog didn't know what they were laughing at, but he felt so well that he laughed too, and Mr. Robin, who had found out by this time what a bad mistake he had made, couldn't help laughing some himself.

Then they had dessert, and Mr. Dog made a speech and thanked them for the fine party and surprise in his honor, and declared he had never spent such a happy day in all his life. He said there had been a little misunderstanding now and then between himself and some of the forest folks, but he knew now that all was forgiven, and that he would never forget this happy May party.

And Mr. Dog never did forget it, concluded the Story Teller—at least not for a long time—and he doesn't know to this day that the party wasn't given specially for him, or that Mr. Jack Rabbit's poem wasn't written in his honor.

"You can sing the Hollow Tree Song, now," said the Little Lady, drowsily.

So then the Story Teller sang the song that the forest people sing when, on dark nights in the far depths of the Deep Woods, they are feasting at the table of the 'Coon, the 'Possum and the Old Black Crow.

Long before he had finished, the Little Lady was in the land of dreams.

And the Story Teller had been dreaming, too, while he sang.

THE HOLLOW TREE SONG.

Oh, there was an old 'Possum in the Big Deep Woods—
As fat as a 'Possum could be—
And he lived in a hollow, hollow,
hollow, hollow, hollow,
He lived in a hollow tree.

Oh, there was an old Coon in the Big Deep Woods—
As sly as a 'Coon could be—
And he lived in a hollow, hollow,
hollow, hollow, hollow,
He lived in a hollow tree.

Oh, there was an old Crow in the Big Deep Woods—
As black as a Crow could be—
And he lived in a hollow, hollow,
hollow, hollow, hollow,
He lived in a hollow tree.

For they all lived together in the Big Deep Woods,
As you can plainly see,
And the 'Possum made one, and the 'Coon made two,
And the Old Black Crow made three.

Then here's to the 'Possum, and the Old Black Crow,
And the 'Coon, with a one, two, three!
And here's to the hollow, hollow,
hollow, hollow, hollow,
And here's to the hollow tree.

THE LITTLE LADY'S VACATION AND HER RETURN

The Little Lady who lives in the House of Many Windows (sometimes called a flat or an apartment by people who, because they are grown up, do not know any better) had been spending the summer on a nice farm in the Land of Pleasant Fields. There had been many things to see—little pigs among other things, and some very small chickens. Also a cow with two calves—one a dark red one, and one spotted, even to its tail, that looked like a barber pole.

Amid all this, and a great deal more, not forgetting the Hillside of Sweet Fruits, the Little Lady had almost forgotten a number of people who lived in the Big Deep Woods, and whose acquaintance she had made through the Story Teller during the winter before, while sailing at evening in the Rockaby Chair for the Shore of White Pillows.

But when the cold winds began to blow and they were all back to the City of Rumbling Streets in the House of Many Windows again and she heard the wind men moaning in the speaking tube, she forgot even the striped tailed calf, and remembered all at once the dark forest and the queer people who dwelt there. And when the Story Teller that night had drawn his chair up before the fire and sat rocking she climbed upon his knee and rocked, too, while he thought, and smoked, and looked into the blaze.

The Little Lady waited a good while. Then she took hold of the lapel of his coat and tugged it gently and looked up into the Story Teller's face.

"Tell me a story," she commanded softly. "One about Mr. Crow and Mr. 'Possum, and Mr. Jack Rabbit and all the others. What did they do this summer? You know; tell it."

The Story Teller grumbled something about not having met any of these fellows lately, and rocked a little harder and thought very fast.

"I s'pose you've heard about Mr. Crow's April fool," he said, as he knocked the ashes from his pipe into the grate.

"No, I haven't—not that story—I never heard that story," she said eagerly.

So, then, the Story Teller rocked some more, and half shut his eyes and began.

THE STORY OF THE C. X. PIE

MR. CROW PLANS AN APRIL FIRST PARTY AND PREPARES A SURPRISE FOR THE OCCASION

TOLD THE 'COON AND 'POSSUM ABOUT IT RIGHT AWAY.

Once upon a time when the Crow and the 'Coon and the 'Possum lived together in three big hollow branches of a great Hollow Tree in the Big Deep Woods, and used to meet and have good times together in the parlor down stairs, the Crow made up his mind to have a party next day. He told the 'Coon and the 'Possum about it right away, and they asked him if he was going to have Mr. Dog this time, and Mr. Crow said "No" and looked foolish, because once he did have Mr. Dog just for a joke and got the worst of it himself.

"I remember about that," said the Little Lady.

HE WALKED BACK AND FORTH A
WHILE IN HIS OWN ROOM.

That's what the Crow did, too—remembered, and he had never felt just right about the way he had been fooled when he meant to fool the others. So when they reminded him about Mr. Dog he said to himself that he would fool them yet, and he'd do it at this very party.

But he made b'lieve he was very meek and said he was going to have Mr. Jack Rabbit over, and Mr. Turtle, to make a full table, and that they would have chicken pie and hot biscuits with maple syrup for dinner. This suited the 'Coon and the 'Possum exactly, for Mr. Crow was the best cook anywhere in the country, and they were both fond of good things. The 'Coon said he'd go right away with the invitation for Jack Rabbit, and the 'Possum said that he felt like taking a walk anyway, and that he'd pass around by the Wide Blue Water where Mr. Turtle lived, and tell him. So off they went and left Mr. Crow all alone to think about it and get ready.

He walked back and forth a while in his own room and scratched his head, and then he went down stairs out in the sun and thought some more. All at once he jumped right straight up and laughed, for he happened to remember that it was the last day of March, and that it was the very thing to have a party on April fool day, and fool the 'Possum and the 'Coon in some way, so that the others would laugh and say it was the best joke of the season. Then he thought of a way to fool them, and pretty soon he had that fixed, too.

WENT RIGHT TO COOKING AND BAKING.

He didn't wait a minute, but went right to cooking and baking just as hard as ever he could, and pretty soon he had three chicken pies done, as fine looking as any you ever saw. And two of them were fine, sure enough—just as fine as Mr. Crow could make them—but the other wasn't chicken at all. It was made out of leaves and sticks, and the only thing good about it was the crust. This pie he intended for the 'Coon and the 'Possum, and one of the good ones was for Mr. Rabbit and Mr. Turtle. The last one was for himself, with an extra piece over for anybody that might happen to want a second helping.

STOOD AND LOOKED AT THEM.

Well, he set them all in a row on the kitchen table, and walked up and down looking at them and laughing and thinking what fun it would be for the others when Mr. 'Possum and Mr. 'Coon cut their pie and tried to eat what was inside of it. He had the pies set on the table so he knew just which was which, and besides had made some letters on the upper crust so the right ones would be sure to get them. On the leaf pie he had "P. C.," for 'Possum and 'Coon. On one of the others he had "R. T.," for Rabbit and Turtle. On the last one he had "C. X.," which stood for Crow, and an extra piece for manners. He had put these letters where the fancy thing is in the centre of pies, and had joined them together so you'd hardly notice them at first.

All at once, while he was looking at them and laughing, he heard Mr. 'Coon and Mr. 'Possum coming back. Then he called out to them and asked them if they had invited the guests and told them to come up and see the pies he had made while they were gone. So they came up and looked at them, and said they certainly were fine, and that Mr. Rabbit and Mr. Turtle were busy getting out their best clothes, and would be there early.

"OH," SAID MR. 'COON, "I HOPE YOU'RE NOT GOING TO CUT THEM."

Then the Crow said he guessed he'd slip over to Mr. Man's pantry and borrow some maple syrup while Mr. Man was at dinner and be back for early supper. So off he went and left the 'Coon and the 'Possum there together.

When he'd been gone awhile Mr. 'Possum said he believed he'd take one more look at those nice pies, and Mr. 'Coon said he guessed he would, too. So they went up to Mr. Crow's kitchen again and stood and looked at them till they were so hungry that Mr. 'Possum licked out his tongue and walked up and smelled of them. First he smelled a good long smell of the C. X. pie—so—and said, "O-o-oh! How nice!" Then he smelled a very long smell of the R. T. pie—so——and said, "O-o-o-o-oh! How delicious!" Then he smelled a very, very long smell of the P. C. pie—so————and said, "O-o-o-o-o-oh! How strange!"

That made the 'Coon want to smell, too, and when he had smelled of all three he said that there certainly did seem to be a difference in those pies, and that the last one had a sort of a woodsy spring-like flavor, like the first of April. That made the 'Possum jump, and he said he had not remembered till that very minute that to-morrow was the first, sure enough. Then he said he didn't suppose Mr. Crow would care how the pies were set on the table, so he moved them about and put the P. C. pie where the C. X. pie had stood, and the C. X. pie at the end instead of the P. C. pie. But while he was doing it he happened to notice the joined letters in the middle of the pies, which he hadn't seen before. He looked at first one and then the other, and studied a minute what to do. Then he picked up an old thin knife that Mr. Crow used for cutting around cake and slipping pies out sometimes when they stuck to the pan.

"Oh," said Mr. 'Coon. "I hope you're not going to cut them!"

"Well," said Mr. 'Possum, "Not so's you'll notice it."

Then he slipped the thin knife around the top crust of the P. C. pie and lifted it off carefully and looked in and made a very queer face. Mr. 'Coon came and looked in, too, and made another very queer face. Then Mr. 'Possum lifted off the top of the C. X. pie and looked in and smiled, and Mr. 'Coon looked in and smiled, too. There were two nice, fat chicken legs right on top, and Mr. 'Coon took one and Mr. 'Possum the other, because they said that as this was to be their pie any way, they might just as well have a little taste of it beforehand. Then they changed the covers and put the P. C. cover on the good pie and C. X. cover on the fool pie, and just then they heard Mr. Crow coming home, and slipped down into the parlor and up into their own rooms and pretended to be asleep when he came in.

THE STORY OF THE C. X. PIE

CONTINUED

MR. CROW'S PARTY AND THE OPENING OF THE PIES

MR. RABBIT CAME IN CARRYING A LARGE BUNCH OF EARLY FLOWERS.

Well, next morning Mr. Crow was down stairs bright and early, putting the big parlor room in order and setting the table. Pretty soon the 'Coon and 'Possum came down, too, and helped him, and now and then, when they happened to look at each other across the table, they would wink and smile, but they didn't say a word. By and by the three pies were brought in and set in a row at one end of the table, and nobody could tell from looking at them but what they were exactly as the Crow had baked them.

MR. TURTLE HIMSELF WADDLED
IN.

Just then there was a knock down stairs, and Mr. Rabbit came in carrying a large bunch of early flowers that he had gathered as he came along, and dressed in his new spring suit. They saw a little white roll in one of his coat pockets, too, and they knew it was a poem for the occasion, for Jack Rabbit writes poems whenever he gets a chance, specially in the early springtime.

Mr. Crow hurried out and got the pair of pink glass vases that Mr. 'Coon had given him for Christmas and put the flowers in them for the table, while he asked Jack Rabbit if it was muddy walking and if he had seen anything of Mr. Turtle.

LEFT THE OTHERS TO SIT AROUND THE
TABLE AND TALK.

Mr. Rabbit said that the ground was rather damp, but that he could pick his way pretty well, and that he had never seen such a wet spring since the year that the Wide Blue Water came up over his back garden and drowned his early pease. He hadn't seen Mr. Turtle, but just then Mr. Turtle himself waddled in with a basket of nice water salad, which he had gathered before starting. Then Mr. Crow hurried off to put his biscuits in the oven and left the others to sit around the table and talk.

After they had talked about the weather and told the latest things that had happened to Mr. Dog, who lived with Mr. Man, and whom none of them liked very well, the 'Possum said all at once that being this was April First he shouldn't wonder if it was to be a sort of surprise party in some way.

That made Mr. Turtle and Jack Rabbit curious right away, and they wanted to know what kind of a surprise he thought it was going to be and if he thought it would be a pleasant one. Mr. 'Possum said he was sure it would be pleasant, and then he looked at the three fine pies on the table and said it was just as apt to be in one of those pies as anywhere. Then Mr. Turtle said he'd heard of "four and twenty blackbirds baked in a pie," and how they began to sing when the pie was opened, but he hoped it wouldn't be that kind of a surprise, for he didn't care much for blackbirds himself, specially in pies. The 'Possum said there might be one black bird sing when these pies were opened, but he didn't b'lieve there'd be any more, which made the 'Coon laugh so he nearly fell off his chair. Just then they heard the Crow coming, and the 'Possum whispered quick to the Turtle and the Rabbit that they must be sure and eat their pie all up and ask for more, as Mr. Crow was proud of his cooking and always felt offended when people didn't eat heartily.

Well, Mr. Crow came in carrying a great pan of fine biscuits and set them down in the middle of the table, while everybody said, "What lovely biscuits!" and asked whether they were made with buttermilk or baking powder, and wanted his recipe. Mr. Crow said he didn't have any recipe, but just took a pinch of this and a pinch of that, and that there was a good deal in the knack and in having things come natural, just as it was natural for Mr. Rabbit to write poetry. Then he said he hoped Mr. Rabbit hadn't forgotten to think up a few thoughts for this occasion, and Mr. Rabbit said that he had been too busy with spring work to write much lately,

74

but that he did have a few lines in his pocket that they might be willing to listen to. So then he took out the roll he had brought and put on his glasses and stood up, while all the others sat still and listened.

Oh, sweet the month of April,
When birds begin to twitter!
When dewdrops on the clover
And tender grasses glitter!
When every shoot of lettuce
That from the ground arises
Gives promise of a salad—
Oh, month of sweet surprises!

You see Mr. Rabbit is a great gardener, and specially fond of young clover and tender salad.

Oh, sweet the month of April,
When youthful chicks are hatching,
And gayly in the meadows
Around their ma are scratching!
The finest way to eat them
In dumpling or in pies is—
Oh, here's to you, sweet April,
With all your glad surprises!

Mr. Rabbit knew that the Crow would have chicken either in dumpling or pies, and anyhow he needed "pies is" to rhyme with "surprises," and when he came to those lines and sat down the others shouted and laughed and Mr. Crow pounded on the table and declared he couldn't have done better if he'd been a poet and written it himself! And the 'Coon and the 'Possum both pounded too and said "That's so! That's so!"

Then Mr. Crow shoved the R. T. pie over between Jack Rabbit and Mr. Turtle and the pie that was marked P. C. between the 'Coon and the 'Possum. The C. X. pie he pulled up in front of himself, for of course he never even suspected that the top crust on them had been changed by the 'Possum.

The finest way to eat them
In dumpling or in pies is—

he said, quoting Mr. Rabbit's poem,

Oh, here's to you, sweet April,
With all your glad surprises!

Then he told them not to be bashful, but to help themselves and remember there was plenty more where that came from. Just as he said this he picked up his knife and stuck it down deep into the C. X. pie. Mr. 'Possum picked up his knife and stuck it down deep into the P. C. pie, and Mr. Rabbit picked up his knife and stuck it into the R. T. pie and cut it in half. Mr. Turtle was watching him pretty anxiously, for he remembered what the 'Possum had said about a surprise, but when Jack Rabbit laid a smoking half with the gravy running out of it on his plate he forgot all about everything else.

THEN, ALL OF A SUDDEN, HE DIDN'T WANT TO LAUGH ANY MORE.

Mr. 'Possum didn't divide the P. C. pie just yet, but kept cutting as if it cut very hard, and talking a good deal while he cut. He said that, speaking of surprises, it used to be quite a fashion to fool people on the first of April, and that he'd known lots of the biggest kind of jokes played on people that day. The biggest jokes, though, he said, were those that came back on the people who played them, and that he knew one of that kind once that made him laugh now every time he thought about it. Then he did laugh some, and sawed away and said he guessed he'd struck a bone; and the 'Coon laughed, too, and Mr. Crow was nearly dying with trying to keep from laughing, for he thought Mr. 'Possum was sawing away on an old stick. He didn't want to let on, though, so he quit looking and commenced cutting his own pie. He laughed to himself and cut a minute, and then, all of a sudden, he didn't want to laugh any more, for he had cut a hole in the top of the C. X. pie and he saw something and smelled something that made him right sick. He looked over quick to Mr. 'Possum's plate, and what he saw there made him sicker yet. For there lay a half of the P. C. pie, and Mr. Crow saw with one look that it was just as fine a chicken pie as ever came out of an oven.

Mr. 'Coon had a piece on his plate, too, and they were saying what a fine pie it was, and Mr. Turtle and Mr. Rabbit said so, too, and that Mr. Crow was certainly the finest cook in those parts.

THE STORY OF THE C. X. PIE

CONTINUED

WHAT HAPPENS TO MR. CROW AND HIS PIE

Poor Mr. Crow! You never saw anybody look as sickly and foolish as he did. He thought that he had made a dreadful mistake in marking the pies, and that now he had got to eat or pretend to eat the mess of old leaves and sticks that filled up the C. X. pie clear to the top. He never thought of Mr. 'Possum's changing the crust, and even if he had, he wouldn't have felt any better.

I DON'T SUPPOSE YOU'LL EVER KNOW JUST HOW BAD MR. CROW DID FEEL.

I don't suppose you'll ever know just how bad Mr. Crow did feel, unless you get into a fix like that some time yourself. First he got hot and then he got cold, and the sweat began to break out on his bill like dew drops. He began to eat a little of the crust first, and then he was afraid if he ate the crust away the others would see what was inside of it, so he put his fork in and got a rolled up leaf with gravy on it and whisked it into his mouth and chewed and tried to swallow till his eyes stuck out and the tears ran down in a stream. He was glad that nobody seemed to be looking at him, for everybody else was too busy eating the nice pie, and Mr. 'Possum was just saying that he liked Mr. Crow's surprises, for he always surprised them by having something better than they expected.

Then he told how once, when they were snowed in, Mr. Crow had kept them all from starving by making a kind of bread called Johnnie cake, and some chicken gravy, and how they could never get him to tell where he got the things to make it of. He said he thought maybe Mr. Crow would tell pretty soon, though, now. Then they all looked at Mr. Crow and begged him to tell his great secret, and when they looked they saw he wasn't eating his pie, but was just sitting there picking at it with his fork a little. They all told him not to be afraid to eat some of his own nice pie, for they were sure there'd be plenty, and Mr. Crow said in a weakly voice that when he cooked he never could eat very much. He said he guessed he'd take a biscuit and some syrup because he didn't feel quite well, anyway. So he pushed the C. X. pie away and ate a biscuit with butter and syrup on it, and felt a good deal better.

But pretty soon Mr. Turtle finished his piece and remembered what Mr. 'Possum had whispered about asking for a second helping. So he said he guessed he'd take another piece of that fine pie—just a small one to hold the other down. Mr. Rabbit said he guessed he'd have to ask for another small piece, too, it was so good, and the

78

Coon and the 'Possum both said that, although they were home folks and used to Mr. Crow's good cooking, they certainly would have to take another little piece of that fine pie.

FAINTED DEAD AWAY.

Then Mr. Crow knew there were only two things that he could do. He could either faint, or "holler" "Fire!" And, after studying for about half a second, he keeled right over and fainted dead away.

Of course that stopped the dinner for a while. Jack Rabbit and Mr. Turtle jumped up frightened, and the 'Coon and the 'Possum pretended to be frightened, too. They all ran to Mr. Crow and carried him up stairs to his room and put him on his bed. Then Mr. 'Coon brought some water and Mr. Rabbit fanned him and Mr. Turtle unbuttoned his vest to give him air. Mr. 'Possum he stood still and gave orders, and said pretty soon that he was sure a good strong hot mustard poultice would help matters. When he said that Mr. Crow opened his eyes a little pinch and asked where he was, and then he said he guessed he must have fainted, for he'd been taken with a dreadful bad turn at the table and didn't remember any more.

Mr. 'Possum winked at Mr. 'Coon and said yes, that Mr. Crow had even forgot to give them a second helping of pie, but that he supposed Mr. Rabbit and Mr. Turtle could go back and help themselves. Then the sweat broke out on Mr. Crow again, and he said he hoped they wouldn't, for it would be cold now and they would find the biscuits and syrup much better. Jack Rabbit said he thought so, too, and the 'Possum, who was really beginning to feel sorry for the poor Crow, said the same, and so did the others. So then Mr. Crow got better as quick as anything, and they all went back down stairs and ate the biscuits and syrup, which were certainly very fine. Once Mr. Rabbit wondered what that nice, leafy smell was that he got a whiff of now and then, and Mr. Turtle said he'd been thinking about that, too. Then Mr. 'Coon helped out and said that he s'posed it was Mr. Man and Mr. Dog burning brush over on the edge of the Wide Grass Lands, and he went on to make a little speech that was kind of a reply to Mr. Rabbit's poem. He said how nice it was to give one's friends pleasant surprises of good things as Mr. Crow had done, instead of unpleasant ones such as Mr. 'Possum had mentioned, and all the others said, "Yes, Yes!" and cheered him, all except Mr. Crow, who looked down into his plate and didn't say a word, but just seemed to be thinking and thinking.

And by and by, when Jack Rabbit and Mr. Turtle said goodby and went away, he hurried back to the table, and was just going to take the C. X. pie up to his own part of the house, when Mr. 'Possum and Mr. 'Coon grabbed him and said they must have a piece of that pie, after all. And when Mr. Crow wasn't going to give it to them they both commenced to laugh and said it was their pie anyway, and that they meant to have it. And right then Mr. Crow knew just what had happened, and that it was no use to be an April fool any longer. He stood still a minute, looking first at Mr. 'Coon and then at Mr. 'Possum. Then he walked to the window and flung the C. X. pie out as far as he could send it among the leaves and brush, where it belonged. The 'Coon stood on one side and the 'Possum on the other, and they watched it strike and roll out of sight before they said anything. Then Mr. 'Coon said that perhaps it would be a good time now to tell the great secret of the Johnnie cake and gravy, and Mr. Crow said he would do that and anything else they wanted him to if they'd promise they wouldn't tell this joke on him to anybody—Mr. Rabbit and Mr. Turtle especially. Then he went right on and told them the great secret of the Johnnie cake, and the 'Coon and the 'Possum did promise, though they didn't intend to tell anyway, for they thought a great deal of Mr. Crow and they were all good friends.

"But, dear me!" exclaimed the story teller, "I've been telling for three evenings on this story, and here it is nine o'clock again."

"You'll tell some more to-morrow night won't you?" said the Little Lady, drowsily.

"We'll have a story about Mr. Jack Rabbit next time," said the story teller.

MR. RABBIT EXPLAINS

AN EASTER STORY

"Now tell me the rabbit story," commanded the Little Lady on the next evening. "You know you promised to."

"So I did," said the Story Teller, "and it goes this way:—"

"One afternoon in the early spring Mr. Jack Rabbit and his friends were out for an airing. The Hollow Tree people were along, and Mr. Turtle, as usual. By and by they came to a log under a big tree and sat down for a smoke and talk. They talked about the weather at first and other things, till somebody mentioned Easter. Then they all had something to say about that.

"'What I object to,' says Mr. Rabbit, when it came his time to talk, 'is this thing of people always saying that the Easter eggs belong to me.'

"'Oh, but that's just a joke,' says Mr. 'Coon, laughing.

"'I know it's just a joke, of course, but it's a pretty old joke, and I'm tired of it,' says Jack Rabbit.

"'How did it get started anyway?' asked Mr. 'Possum.

"Then Mr. Rabbit took his pipe out of his mouth and leaned forward a little, so he could talk better.

"'I tell you how it got started,' he says, 'and after that I don't want to hear any more of it. This is how it happened:—

"'Once upon a time, as much as twenty grandmothers back, I should think, there was a very nice family of Rabbits that lived in a grassy place on a hillside back of a big farmyard. There was quite a hole in the ground there, and they had a cosy home in it, and a soft bed for their little folk."

A FEW LESSONS IN RUNNING AND HIDING.

IT WAS A NICE BLUE EGG WHEN SHE GOT THROUGH.

"'Now, every bright morning, Father and Mother Rabbit used to take the children out for a walk, and for a few lessons in running and hiding from Mr. Dog, who bothered about a good deal, and one day as they were coming home they heard a great cackling, and when they got to their house there was a nice fresh egg lying right in the children's bed. Some old hen from the farmyard had slipped in and laid it while they were gone. A good many hens, especially old hens, like to hide their nests that way, and this was one of that kind.

"'Well, of course all the young Rabbits claimed it, and Mother Rabbit at last gave it to the smallest and weakest one of the children, a little girl, who was always painting things with the juice of flower petals. And the very first thing that little girl did was to stain that egg all over with violet juice, not thinking what trouble it was going to cause our family forever after.

"'It was a nice blue egg when she got through with it, and the next day, when they all came back from their walk again there was another white egg right by it. The old hen had been there again and laid another while they were gone. The second little girl claimed that egg, of course, and she painted it a bright yellow with buttercup juice. Then the next day there was another egg, and the next day there was another egg, and the next day there was another egg, until there was one apiece for every one of the children, and some over.'"

"'And they all painted them. Some painted theirs pink or red with roseleaves or japonica, some painted them yellow with buttercups, and some blue or purple with violets, as the first little girl had done. They had so many at last that it crowded them out of their bed, and they had to sleep on the floor.

"'And then, one Sunday, and it must have been Easter Sunday, they all went out walking again, and when they came back every one of those beautiful colored eggs was gone. The children cried and made a great fuss, but it was no use. Some of Mr. Man's boys out hunting hen's nests had found them and taken them all home with them.

"'And of course all those colored eggs set Mr. Man to wondering, and he came with his boys to the place where they had found them; and when they looked in out jumped the whole Rabbit family, helter skelter in every direction."

LEANING OVER TO LIGHT HIS PIPE FROM MR. 'POSSUM'S.

"'And right then,' said Mr. Rabbit, leaning over to light his pipe from Mr. 'Possum's, 'right then Mr. Man declared those colored eggs were rabbit eggs, and he's kept on saying so ever since, though he knows better, and he knows I don't like it. He takes eggs and colors them himself now, and makes believe they're mine, and he puts my picture all over things about Easter time. I suppose he thinks I don't care, but I do, and I wish that little Miss Rabbit twenty grandmothers back had left that old hen's egg white as she found it.'

"'It's too bad,' says Mr. Crow. 'It's like that story they tell about the fox making me drop the cheese.'

"'Or like Mr. Man making believe that the combs he uses are really made out of my shell,' says Mr. Turtle.

"Mr. 'Coon and Mr. 'Possum shook their heads. They had their troubles, too."

MR. TURTLE'S THUNDER STORY

THE WAY OF THE FIRST THUNDER AND LIGHTNING

84

HAD JACK RABBIT AND MR. TURTLE IN FOR SUPPER.

Once upon a time, said the Story Teller, when the Crow and the 'Coon and the 'Possum lived together in three big, hollow branches of a big big, hollow tree in the big, big, Big Deep Woods, and used to meet and have good times together in the parlor down stairs, they had Jack Rabbit and Mr. Turtle in for supper. It was a nice supper, too, for it was just about strawberry time, and strawberries grow thicker in the Big Deep Woods than fur on a kitten's back. Mr. Crow, who is a great cook, had made a nice shortcake, and been over to Mr. Man's pantry, where he gets some of his best things, and borrowed a pail of sweet cream when Mr. Man wasn't at home.

"Of course they had fried chicken, too, first, and by the time they were through their shortcake and had lit their pipes Mr. 'Possum, who likes good things better than anybody, almost, could hardly open his eyes. He said he wished he was a poet, like Mr. Jack Rabbit, for he had never been so full of summer happiness since he was born, and if he could only make rhymes, he knew that poetry would slip right off his tongue. Then, of course, Mr. Rabbit wanted to show off, and without stopping a second he commenced to talk poetry—this way:—

"In the summer time I make a rhyme
For every breeze that passes,
For I can always make it chime
With lassies, grasses, sasses."

"Mr. 'Possum said he couldn't do that if it was to save him from being hung the next minute, and Mr. Rabbit went right on without catching his breath:—

"Where e'er I go my verses flow—
I keep it up for hours.

85

I'm never short of rhymes, you know,
With bowers, flowers, showers."

"Well, that set them all to wondering how Jack Rabbit could do it so easily, and Mr. Rabbit didn't think to tell them how he'd sat up all the night before to compose this poetry, so's to have it on hand and ready for a chance to use it. He said that it was somebody else's turn now, and that maybe Mr. Turtle would give them a performance of some kind. Mr. Turtle wanted to change the subject, and got up and walked over to the window. He said that, speaking of showers, it was so warm and close, he shouldn't wonder if they had one before morning. He said he believed there was lightning now, off in the west, and seemed like he could hear it thunder, too. Then they all talked about thunder and lightning and what they were. But nobody seemed to know except Mr. Turtle himself.

"'Why,' he said, 'I thought everybody knew that!' Then he went on to say that he'd known the story ever since he wasn't 'any bigger than a pants button,' and all the others said he must tell it to them, because it was his turn, anyway. And Mr. Turtle was glad to do that, for he really wanted to show off a little, like Jack Rabbit, only he hadn't known before how to do it. So he filled up his pipe nice and fresh, and lit it, and began.

"'Well,' he said, 'of course you know my family all live to be pretty old. I'm only three hundred and sixteen next spring myself, but Uncle Tom Turtle, who lives up by the forks, is a good deal over nine hundred, and he isn't nearly as old as Father Storm Turtle and his wife, who live up in the Big West Hills, and make the thunder and lightning.'

"Mr. Turtle stopped a minute to light his pipe again, and all the others just looked at him and couldn't say a word. They knew he was pretty old, but they had never thought much about it before, and what he said about Father and Mother Storm Turtle they had never even heard of. But Mr. Turtle just lit his pipe, and puffed, and said:—

"'To tell the truth, I never did hear of any of our family dying of old age, and I shouldn't wonder if Old Man Turtle Himself would still be alive, too, if he hadn't tried to swallow a mussel fish with the shell on and got it stuck in his throat a million and twenty-five years ago last spring. Anyhow, that's according to the date cut on his shell overcoat that Uncle Tom Turtle saw once at Father Storm's house up in the Big West Hills.

"'I don't know how many great grandfathers back Father Storm is from me, nor how many from Father Storm Old Man Turtle Himself was, but I know Father Storm got his shell overcoat after the mussel fish wouldn't go down, and that it was a great deal too big to take in the house, and it used to set out in the yard on four bricks, for the children to play under.

"'Father Storm Turtle had a big family then, and they were pretty troublesome. They had a habit of wandering off in the woods and forgetting to come back. Every night Mother Storm had to stand in the door and call and call and not be able to sleep if they didn't come, especially when it was cloudy and looked like rain. She knew that, if they got wet they'd all come home with bad colds and sore throats and make trouble and expense. Three of them—named Slop, Splash and Paddle—were worse than any of the others, for even when it didn't rain they were always playing in dirty puddles, and would come home all mud and with wet feet.'"

MR. TURTLE'S THUNDER STORY

CONTINUED

FATHER STORM'S PLAN AND HOW IT WORKED

"At last, one day, when Mother Storm Turtle had shouted herself hoarse and couldn't make any of them hear, she said she wouldn't put up with it any longer, and that Father Storm had got to fix up some way to call those children home when she wanted them, especially when it was going to rain, as it was now. So Father Storm went out into the front yard and sat down and looked at the clouds and thought and thought."

WENT RIGHT TO WORK AND DUG TWO HOLES.

"All at once, just as he was about to give it up, he happened to be looking right at the shell of Old Man Turtle Himself. He jumped up quick and hit it with his cane, and when it made quite a loud sound he laughed, for he knew, now, how he could make those children hear when he wanted them. He didn't say a word to Mother Storm Turtle, but went right to work and dug two holes and put up two tall posts in the yard and fastened a stout beam across the top of them. Then he worked until he had bored a hole in one end of the shell of Old Man Turtle Himself, and put a chain in it and dragged it over and strung it up between the posts, so that it swung there and didn't quite touch the ground. That, of course, made a thing a good deal like Mr. Man's dinner gong, only a hundred times as big, and about a thousand times as loud. Then Father Storm went out into the woodhouse to make a club to beat it with, laughing to himself now and then when he thought how Mother Storm Turtle would most have a fit when she heard it for the first time.

"But while Father Storm Turtle was doing so much, Mother Storm had been thinking and doing some herself. She was getting supper, and when she looked into the fire to put in a stick of wood, she just happened to think that if she could make a torch big enough and bright enough, when she stood in the door and waved it, those children would see the light, especially nights when it was dark just before a heavy rain. So she went right to work and made one, just as big as she could make it, and put lots of oil and fat on it, to make it bright. She laughed to think how Father Storm Turtle would jump when she waved that out the door, and how the children would come running when they saw the big flash. Then she noticed that it was getting darker and darker and would rain in a minute. So she hurried up and lit it and stepped to the door and gave it a great big swing. And just that second Father Storm hit the shell of Old Man Turtle Himself with a big hickory club, and there was never such a light nor such a roar in the world as that was.

"Mother Storm Turtle tumbled over backward and set the house afire with her torch, and Father Storm was so frightened by the big light that at first he couldn't help her put the fire out. And just then it began raining like forty, and all the children came running and screaming out of the woods, half scared to death by the big light and noise. It made a terrible commotion there for a few minutes, until they got the fire put out, and people heard it all over the country, even to Mr. Man's house. And when they found out what it was, and who started it, everybody called it a 'storm.' And rain and wind and thunder and lightning, or most any other kind of a big fuss, is called a 'storm' to this day, after Father and Mother Storm Turtle."

SLOP AND SPLASH AND PADDLE.

"And that," said Mr. Turtle, lighting his pipe once more, "was the first thunder and lightning, and whenever people saw it after that they said, 'We're going to have another storm!' For Father and Mother Storm Turtle went right on using the big torch and the shell of Old Man Turtle Himself to call in the children just before a rain, and the children would come running every time, all except Slop, Splash and Paddle, who got so at last that they liked the mud and dirty water better than anything else. They liked the mud so well that Father Storm told them one day they might go and live in the mud and be named Mud for all he cared; and so they did, and their names were Mud, and they and all their families live in dirty water and are called Mud Turtles to this day. They never went home again, but whenever they hear Father Storm pounding on the shell, they stop whatever they are doing and listen. And that's how the saying began that 'a Mud Turtle never lets go till it thunders.'"

"What makes the noise always get louder and the light brighter just before it rains?" asked Jack Rabbit.

"Why, you see," said Mr. Turtle, "Father and Mother Storm's grandchildren and great-grandchildren are a good deal scattered now, and as the old people run the thunder and lightning mostly on their account, they try to make it just about bright enough and loud enough to keep up with the rain wherever it goes."

"It's plenty loud enough," said Mr. 'Coon solemnly.

"And plenty bright enough," said Mr. Crow, blinking.

"What makes it set things on fire sometimes?" asked Mr. 'Possum sleepily.

"That's when Mother Storm Turtle swings her torch too hard and coals fly out of it," said Mr. Turtle, as he got up and walked over to the window.

Then the Crow and the 'Coon and the 'Possum and Jack Rabbit got up, too, and walked over, and they all looked out together. It was dark among the trees below them, and Mr. Turtle pointed off toward the Big West Hills.

"You see," he said, speaking low, "Mother Storm is beginning to swing her torch, and you'll hear Father Storm pounding before long on the shell of Old Man Turtle Himself."

So the five friends stood very still and listened and pretty soon they did hear a low far off rumble, sure enough.

"That means it's time to start for home," said Mr. Jack Rabbit, reaching for his hat and cane.

Mr. Turtle reached for his hat and cane, too, and they felt their way down the dim stairs, with Mr. 'Coon holding a candle, and Mr. Crow and Mr. 'Possum looking after them.

"Good night, everybody," said Mr. Turtle.

CALLED TO JACK RABBIT TO PUSH IN THE LATCH.

"Push the latch string in from the outside," called Mr. Crow. "Then, I won't have to come down."

"All right!
Good night!"
called back Jack Rabbit.

"Good night! Come again!" called the Crow and the 'Coon and the 'Possum.

A RAIN IN THE NIGHT

A WINDOW THAT WASN'T CLOSED, AND WHO CLOSED IT

The night was warm in the Hollow Tree. Jack Rabbit and Mr. Turtle, who had been spending the evening with the 'Coon and 'Possum and the Old Black Crow, had hurried off to their homes, so as to get there before the rain set in.

They had all stood by an open parlor window and seen it coming over the Big West Hills, and the visitors knew they'd catch it if they didn't hurry. Mr. Crow and the others had watched them down stairs, and called to Jack Rabbit to push in the latch string, which would fasten the door from the outside. Then Mr. 'Possum had taken his candle, and Mr. 'Coon had taken his candle, and Mr. Crow had taken his candle, and each had gone up to his own room and scrambled into bed quick, so's to be able to cover up his head when it thundered.

Well, they hadn't any more than all gone to bed before Mr. Crow suddenly happened to remember that, being in such a hurry, none of them had thought to close the parlor window, and it would rain in as sure as the world. There was a little table close to the window, with some of his best things on it, too, and if it rained in they would all get wet and be spoiled. He thought about this twice, and maybe more than twice, and the more he thought about it the less he wanted to get up and close that window. Then, all at once, there came a flash of lightning and low growling thunder. Down he bobbed under the covers, and this made him want to get up less than ever. He knew, though, that it would be raining hard pretty soon, and spoiling his things. He had to do something right off.

So, after thinking a minute, he sat up in bed and called out:

"Oh, Mr. 'Coon! You forgot to close the parlor window. It will rain in on your things."

But Mr. 'Coon called back:

"It won't hurt MY things, Mr. Crow. They're over on the other side of the room."

And Mr. 'Possum, who was sitting up in bed, too, listened and laughed in the dark.

But just then there was another flash of lightning, and Mr. Crow bobbed down, and Mr. 'Coon bobbed down, and Mr. 'Possum bobbed down, so's not to hear the thunder. Then, pretty soon, Mr. Crow sat up in bed again and called out:

"Oh, Mr. 'Possum! You forgot to close the parlor window. It will rain in on your things."

But Mr. 'Possum called back:

"It won't hurt MY things, Mr. Crow. They're all over by the stairs."

And Mr. 'Coon, who was sitting up in bed, listened and laughed in the dark, too.

Then for a minute Mr. Crow didn't know but that he'd have to go down and shut that window himself, after all. And while he was thinking how much he didn't want to, there came another flash of lightning, brighter than ever, and Mr. Crow and Mr. 'Coon and Mr. 'Possum all bobbed down again and covered up their heads, so's not to hear the thunder. But Mr. Crow heard it a little, anyway, and it set him to thinking. So when he sat up again he called out:

"Oh, Mr. 'Coon, did Jack Rabbit push in the latch string down stairs?"

And Mr. 'Coon called back:

"I s'pose so, Mr. Crow. You told him to. Why?"

"Oh, nothing, only he left in a great hurry, and I thought maybe he didn't get it quite in."

And Mr. 'Possum listened again, but this time he didn't laugh.

Then Mr. Crow called out to him, too:

"Oh, Mr. 'Possum, did Mr. Rabbit push in the latch string when he left?"

And Mr. 'Possum called back:

"I don't know, Mr. Crow. But you told him to. Why?"

"Oh, nothing; only I heard something just now that sounded like Mr. Dog barking and coming this way."

And Mr. 'Coon listened again, too, but he didn't laugh any this time, either.

And just then there was another flash of lightning, a good deal brighter than any of the other flashes, and down went Mr. Crow again, and down went Mr. 'Coon again, and down went Mr. 'Possum again, so's not to hear it thunder. But they did hear it, even under the bedclothes, and being covered up that way, and thinking about Mr. Dog anyhow, made it sound to them exactly like Mr. Dog's voice barking and growling, and coming closer and closer and closer.

And when Mr. 'Coon and Mr. 'Possum heard that they didn't wait another minute. They just threw back the covers, both of them, and piled out of bed and made a rush for that down stairs door, as if Mr. Dog was right behind them, sure enough. And of course neither one knew the other had started, and when they got to the head of the stairs they bumped together in the dark, and down they went, over and over, to the bottom. There was a little flash of lightning just as they got there, and they saw that Mr. Rabbit had pushed in the latch string after all.

Then they felt foolish, and each began to blame the other for making him fall down stairs, and both of them said they knew all the time the door was fastened, and that they weren't afraid of Mr. Dog, anyway. They'd only got up, they said, to shut the parlor window, and they did shut it, both together, as they came back. Then they ran up to their beds quick, while Mr. Crow, who had been listening all the time, laid down and rolled over and laughed and laughed in the dark.

92

And just then there came another big, bright flash, and down under the covers went all three of them, so's not to hear it thunder. They stayed under a good while that time, and when they put their heads out again the shower had commenced, and the thunder was passing over.

So then, pretty soon, the 'Possum and the 'Coon and the Old Black Crow all dropped off to sleep to the sound of the rain falling among the leaves and branches of the Hollow Tree.

A DEEP WOODS FISHING PARTY

AN ADVENTURE WITH MR. DOG AND A VERY LARGE FISH

One warm June morning, when the sun was trying to shine and couldn't, and the air was close and still and sticky, Mr. Jack Rabbit looked out of the window while he was dressing and thought to himself that it would be just the very morning for fish to bite.

Jack Rabbit liked to fish better than anything, almost, so right after breakfast he took an empty tomato can and went out in the back yard and turned over boards till he had the can about half full of bait, with a little dirt thrown on top. Then he reached up under the eaves of the smoke-house and pulled out a long cane pole with a line and hook and floater on it, all rigged up ready, and flung it over his shoulder and started.

Mr. Rabbit walked pretty fast—even lazy folks do that when they go fishing, and Mr. Jack Rabbit wasn't lazy, by a good deal. So pretty soon he came to the Hollow Tree, and there, looking out of an upstairs window, he saw the 'Coon, the 'Possum and the Old Black Crow.

"Hello, up there!" he said. "Don't you fellows want to go fishing?"

Mr. 'Possum said he thought fish would bite well on such a morning, and that he'd like to go first rate. Mr. 'Coon said he knew a place where you could pull them out as fast as you could throw in your hook, and he went on and told how he caught a fish there last year that would weigh more than four pounds, and lost him just as he got him to the top of the water. Mr. Crow said he'd always noticed that Mr. 'Coon's four pound fish never got any nearer to him than the top of the water, and that for his part he didn't care much about fishing. He said, though, that if the 'Coon and the 'Possum wanted to go he'd stay at home and get dinner while they were gone, so's to have it ready when they all came home hungry. He told them that he had some nice canned salmon in the cupboard that he could catch most any time, and that if they really wanted fish for dinner he s'posed he might as well open it. Then they all laughed, and in about a minute down came Mr. 'Coon and Mr. 'Possum with their fishing things. Jack Rabbit said he had plenty of bait, so away they went. Mr. Crow sat up in the window and watched them off, and Mr. Robin, who happened along just then, laughed and called after them that he'd take a few pounds of nice bass when they got home. The Robin just said that to plague them, of course, and Mr. 'Coon called back that they'd fool him this time, and then he went on to remark to the 'Possum and the Rabbit that he'd never in his life seen a finer day for fishing.

Jack Rabbit said yes, that it was fine, and that it was a fine day for Mr. Dog to be out gallivanting over the country, too, and that they'd better hurry up and get to the lake and out in his boat before anything happened. That made Mr. 'Possum take a good deal livelier step, though he commenced to whistle and said he wasn't afraid of Mr. Dog, anyway. Mr. 'Coon said he'd always noticed that a fellow mostly whistled when he wasn't afraid, but for his part he couldn't get to that boat any too soon. And pretty soon they did get to it, and Mr. 'Possum was the first one to pile in, though Mr. Dog wasn't anywhere in sight.

Well, they pushed off and Jack Rabbit took one oar and Mr. 'Coon the other, while the 'Possum sat on the back seat and baited his hook so's to catch the first fish. Then, when they got out to where Mr. 'Coon said the good place was, they all went to fishing, and Mr. 'Possum did get the first bite, but he didn't get anything else when he pulled. Mr. 'Coon told him he pulled too quick, and Jack Rabbit told him he didn't pull quick enough, and asked him if he expected the fish to climb out on his pole. Then Mr. Rabbit had a bite himself, and pulled and didn't get anything, either. Of course, that made Mr. 'Possum laugh, and then, all at once, the 'Coon had a great big bite that took his float away down out of sight the first grab.

Mr. 'Coon let him go for a minute and then gave a hard pull and commenced to call out that he had him this time and that he'd show Mr. Crow now about only getting fish to the top of the water and having canned salmon for dinner. Then he stood up in the boat and pulled as hard as ever he could till all of a sudden his line broke, and down he went backwards, right on top of Mr. 'Possum, while the Rabbit swung his hook over where the 'Coon's hook had been and the big fish grabbed it before you could say Jack Robinson.

That was too bad for the 'Coon and the 'Possum, of course, and it wasn't as much fun for Jack Rabbit as you might suppose, for he couldn't get the big fish out to save his life, and he had to hold on to the boat to keep from being pulled into the lake. Then he called to the others to help him, and they both got up and took hold of the pole and hauled in hand over hand till they got to the line, and that was as far as they could get. So Mr. Rabbit gave the line a twist or two around the iron ring in the front of his boat, and the big fish started straight for shore, dragging the boat and everybody in it behind him, just as hard as ever he could go. Then Mr. 'Coon and Jack Rabbit commenced to quarrel about whose fish it was, and Mr. 'Possum said he didn't care whose it was, he was getting a free ride, and he laid back and laughed and looked at the shore, when all of a sudden he happened to spy there, sitting on the end of a log, fishing and waiting for them, nobody but Mr. Dog himself.

That wasn't very much, of course, but it was plenty for Mr. 'Possum. He quit laughing and tumbled down in the bottom of the boat and laid there calling for Jack Rabbit to cut that fishline or they'd all be chops and steaks and carried home in a basket in less than five minutes. Jack Rabbit did try to cut the line, too, but he was so excited he dropped his knife overboard, and Mr. 'Coon couldn't find his, and Mr. 'Possum didn't have any. So there they were, and there was Mr. Dog! Then Mr. Rabbit tried to bite the line off with his teeth, but he couldn't do that, either, for it was a big, strong line that he'd made himself, 'specially for big fish.

And all the time they were getting closer and closer to the shore, and Mr. Dog had lifted his line out of the water so it wouldn't be in his way, and was sitting there waiting, and smiling to see them come.

Then Jack Rabbit knew that something had to be done, and there was no time to lose. He was just about as scared as he could be, but he knew it wouldn't do any good to let on, so he sat up straight and smiled some, too, and looked at Mr. Dog and called out, big and friendly like:

"Hello, Mr. Dog! Here we come! Here we come with a nice dinner, Mr. Dog!"

Then Mr. Dog laughed and called back:

"That's right, Mr. Rabbit. There's a sure enough nice dinner coming, this time! Fish for the first course, Mr. Rabbit!"

When Mr. 'Possum heard that he began to groan, and Jack Rabbit and Mr. 'Coon began to shiver, for each thought he knew pretty well what the next courses of Mr. Dog's dinner would be. But Mr. Rabbit didn't stop smiling or let on that he knew, and he called out again to Mr. Dog, quick:

"You'll have to help us if we have fish, Mr. Dog! He's a big one and you'll have to help us catch him!"

And Mr. Dog called back again:

"Don't worry, Mr. Rabbit! I won't leave! I'll be on hand when you get here, Mr. Rabbit!"

Then he rolled up his trousers a little and waded out into the shallow water, thinking he would nab Mr. Fish first and drag him out on shore, and then pull the boat right in after him.

THE FIGHT BETWEEN MR. DOG AND THE BIG FISH.

Of course, that was a pretty good plan for Mr. Dog, only like some other good plans, it didn't work just as he expected it to. You see, he didn't quite know how big the fish was, nor how hard a big fish is to handle in shallow water. He made a quick grab at it when it got to him and then, right away, he had his hands full of business. That fish gave a flop with his tail that laid Mr. Dog over on his back and then another flop that set him on his feet again, and a side flop that smacked him against the water first one way and then the other, and made him breathe hard and choke and try to let go.

But Mr. Dog couldn't let go, for he'd got the fish line some way tangled in his teeth. So he began to snap and paw and swallow water, and fall down and get up again, and sprawl about in the swamp grass, trying to get back to shore.

And while all this was going on Jack Rabbit and his friends had jumped out into the shallow water and took a little roundin's to shore, keeping out of Mr. Dog's way, and made tracks for the top of a hill, where they would be out of danger and see the fun at the same time. Then they all stood up there and watched the fight between Mr. Dog and the big fish, and Jack Rabbit sang out, as loud as ever he could:

"Don't leave, Mr. Dog! Stay with him, Mr. Dog! Hold him to it, Mr. Dog; you've got him! First course, Mr. Dog!"

And Mr. Dog heard Jack Rabbit and got madder and madder every minute, till all of a sudden he got a lick on the side of the head from Mr. Fish's tail that made him see stars and broke the line. And away went the big fish out into deep water, while Mr. Dog crawled back to shore, wet and bruised from head to foot, and most dead.

Then Mr. 'Coon and Mr. 'Possum and Jack Rabbit, standing on top of the hill, gave a great big laugh, all together, and Mr. Rabbit called out:

"How did you like the first course, Mr. Dog?"

That made them all laugh again, and then Mr. 'Coon called out:

"Are you ready for the second course, Mr. Dog?"

And pretty soon Mr. 'Possum he called out:

"Are you ready for a nice roast now, Mr. Dog?"

And that, of course, made them all laugh very loud, for Mr. 'Possum used slang now and then and meant by a "roast" that people would all make fun of Mr. Dog wherever he went; which they did, for a long time.

Even Mr. Robin, who was good friends with Mr. Dog, couldn't help calling out to him, now and then, as he went by:

"Are you ready for the next course, Mr. Dog?"

And Mr. Dog would pretend not to hear and go hurrying by very fast, as if he were out on special and important business for Mr. Man.

THE HOLLOW TREE INN

THE THREE FRIENDS GO INTO BUSINESS

One rainy day when the 'Coon and 'Possum and the Old Black Crow were rummaging about their house in the Big Hollow Tree where they all lived together, they found that above each of their rooms there was a good deal of other room that nobody ever used. That set them to thinking, and pretty soon Mr. 'Possum said it was too bad to let all that good room go to waste, and Mr. 'Coon said yes, it was, and that their house was big enough for a hotel.

Of course he didn't think what he was saying at the time, but it set Mr. Crow to thinking and walking up and down, whistling, and pretty soon he stopped still and looked at the 'Coon and 'Possum.

"I'll do the cookin'," he said, "if you'll get the things to cook."

And right then and there they made up their minds to do it, and early the next morning, while the Old Black Crow was hurrying about inside, getting things ready for business, the 'Coon and the 'Possum nailed up a sign outside, and this is what was on it:

THE HOLLOW TREE INN.

BOARD BY THE DAY OR WEEK.

Then they went inside to help Mr. Crow get ready, and by and by they all sat down and waited for people to come. Mr. 'Coon and Mr. 'Possum felt pretty well, too, for they thought they would have the easiest time. You see, they had always depended on Mr. Crow a good deal, for, besides being a good cook, he was a great hand to provide, and knew more about where to get the best things, and the best time of day or night to get them, than both of the others put together. So he didn't say anything, but dressed up nice and spruce in a clean apron and cooking cap and leaned out of the window, as cooks always do, with his arms folded. By and by along came Mr. Jack Rabbit.

"HELLO!" HE SAID, "WHAT'S THIS?"

"Hello!" he said. "What's this?"

Then he read the sign over and looked at Mr. Crow and asked him if it was a joke. And Mr. Crow said:

"Not much! Come up and see."

So then Mr. Rabbit went up stairs and Mr. 'Coon and Mr. 'Possum showed him through, and Jack Rabbit said that he didn't feel very well this summer, any way, and he believed he'd just shut up his house and come and board a while for a change. He said he guessed he'd take the room above Mr. 'Coon's, because it had a nice south window and a tall looking glass, and that he'd pack up a few things that he needed and come over right away. Then he went home and the 'Coon and 'Possum and the Old Black Crow all shook hands and danced around in a circle to think how well they were going to do, for if Mr. Jack Rabbit came they were sure of having as many others as their house would hold.

And while they were dancing along came Mr. Robin. He read the sign, too, and laughed, and then knocked at the door till Mr. 'Coon came down and let him in. He thought it was a joke at first, like the Rabbit, but when he heard that Jack Rabbit was coming to board he spoke up just as quick as anything and said he'd come, too, and that he'd have his things there before supper time. He took the room over Mr. Crow, because he said he didn't mind the smell of the cooking, and then maybe he'd learn some new receipts. You see, Mr. Crow and Mr. Robin are sort of kinsfolk, and when they have time they often get together and trace back to find out just what relation they are to each other, and that makes them good friends.

Well, Mr. Robin hadn't more'n got out of the house when who should walk in but Mr. Squirrel.

"What's all this about boarders?" said Mr. Squirrel. "I'm looking for a place to spend a month or two myself."

So then they showed him the room above Mr. 'Possum's, and he was so pleased with the view and everything that he paid a week's board in advance to be sure of keeping anybody else from getting it. When he was gone the 'Coon and 'Possum and the Old Black Crow did another dance, and kept saying over and over how rich they'd be and what they would do with all the money. Then they heard somebody laughing outside, and when they looked out there was Mr. Turtle laughing and reading the sign.

"Hello!" he said. "This isn't the first of April."

"No," said Mr. Crow, "it's a boarding house, and a good one. All the best people in the country stop here. Mr. Rabbit, Mr. Robin and Mr. Squirrel. Sorry, Mr. Turtle, but our rooms are all full."

Then Mr. Turtle did look cheap, for he thought he couldn't be in the crowd, and it was the very crowd he liked to associate with. But just then Mr. 'Coon happened to think that they might fit up the big room below the other big room where they all gathered to eat and talk, and Mr. Turtle said that would suit him, exactly, because he was large and heavy and didn't care much about climbing any way. So he hurried off after his things, too, and he wasn't out of sight before here comes Mr. Dog!

Mr. 'Coon and Mr. 'Possum were both looking out the window when he came up, and they jumped back like lightning. You see, they didn't like Mr. Dog worth a cent. Then Mr. Crow came and looked out the window and talked to him. Mr. Dog was just as polite as a basket of chips, and of course that's the politest thing in the world.

"I've just seen Mr. Robin," said Mr. Dog, "and I came to get a room, too."

"Awfully sorry, Mr. Dog, but our rooms are all full," said Mr. Crow.

"Why don't you take down your sign, then?" said Mr. Dog.

"Hotels never take down their signs," said Mr. Crow.

"Hotels are never too full for one more, either," said Mr. Dog. "If you don't let me come in I think I'll wait around here and make a vacancy."

THE HOLLOW TREE INN

CONTINUED
WHAT HAPPENS TO MR. DOG

Now, when Mr. 'Possum and Mr. 'Coon heard that their hair stood up straight, for they knew very well that there'd be two vacant rooms any way if Mr. Dog ever got inside, and two if he stayed where he was, for they happened to think that Mr. Rabbit would be coming along presently, and Mr. Squirrel wouldn't be far behind. So they hurried to the back window and looked out, and sure enough there was Mr. Rabbit coming with his trunk on his shoulder and almost there. At first they were frightened most to death for Mr. Rabbit, and then the 'Coon slipped over and whispered to the Crow to keep Mr. Dog talking as hard as he could, so he wouldn't notice anything. All the time he was doing this the 'Possum was motioning to Jack Rabbit to slip up easy-like with his trunk.

AND UP HE CAME.

So Mr. Rabbit slipped up softly on the other side of the house from Mr. Dog and set his trunk down, and the 'Possum let out a long rope with a hook on it. Jack Rabbit stood up on his trunk and grabbed the hook as soon as he could reach it and hooked it under his arms. Then the 'Coon and the 'Possum pulled and pulled and up he came, and as soon as he was safe they let down the rope and caught the hook in the trunk handle. That was a load for all three of them, and even then they couldn't get it up, and called across to the Crow to come quick and help. So he had to leave Mr. Dog a minute, and when he did that Mr. Dog walked around the tree, and there was the trunk just a few feet from the ground, going up very slowly. That was enough for Mr. Dog. He knew then he'd been fooled, and he was so mad he didn't know what to do.

He took one look at that trunk and made up his mind he wouldn't stand it. So he stepped back a little and made a short run and gave a jump for the trunk, just as high as ever he could.

HE CAUGHT IT AS HE WENT
BY.

But Mr. Dog wasn't very lucky, for instead of landing on the trunk he landed his nose right against one corner of it, and that made him madder than ever. He ran and jumped again harder than before, but this time the trunk was a little higher and Mr. Dog didn't quite hit it. There was a strap hanging down, though, and he caught it as he went by. He caught it with his teeth, and two of his teeth went right through two of the holes where the buckle catches, and there they stayed. He had the trunk all right enough, but the trunk had him, too.

THE ARRIVAL OF THE OTHER GUESTS.

There he was. His feet didn't quite touch the ground, and he couldn't get up any higher either. Then all at once the people up stairs saw how it was, and they commenced to laugh in spite of themselves, and hitched the rope around a peg under the sill so they could rest a minute. That was fun for them, but it wasn't for Mr. Dog, by a good deal. He couldn't laugh, and he couldn't rest, either. And just then Mr. Squirrel came with his trunk, and Mr. Robin with his satchel and a hand bag, and Mr. Turtle with his things in a big sack. Mr. 'Coon ran down and let them all in and locked the door. Then he ran back to the window where Mr. Dog was.

"If we'll let you down will you go home and not come around this hotel interfering with our business?" says Mr. 'Possum.

"Yes; will you promise not to try to get any of our guests away from us?" says Mr. 'Coon.

Mr. Dog couldn't talk much in the fix he was in, but he did the best he could, and promised yes to everything, so pretty soon, they let the trunk down till his feet touched the ground, and he could get his teeth out of the strap. Then he put out for home just about as fast as he could go, without so much as thanking them for letting him down, and up went Mr. Rabbit's trunk pretty quick, now that there were plenty to help.

Then the guests all hurried to their rooms to unpack, and Mr. Crow bustled around to get supper with what he had in the house, for Mr. 'Possum and Mr. 'Coon hadn't time yet to bring in anything. It was a pretty good supper, though, and all the guests said so, and said they knew what a good cook Mr. Crow was if he had things to work with, and the Crow said he guessed he could do his part if the 'Coon and 'Possum would do theirs.

Well, it makes a good deal of difference whether you're company at a house or a boarder. They all felt a good deal like company at first, but by the next evening at supper time they felt different. Mr. 'Coon and Mr. 'Possum had been out all day bringing in things, too, and Mr. Crow had been cooking harder than ever. Mr. Robin was first to make remarks. He said that the cherries were canned, and not very good ones at that.

"That's what I said," put in Mr. 'Coon, "but Mr. 'Possum said you wouldn't know the difference."

101

"Oh, he did, did he?" says Mr. Robin. "Well, I've got better cherries than these at home," and he got up from the table with a disgusted air.

Then Mr. Squirrel picked up some roasted nuts that the Crow had just brought in.

"Where'd you get these nuts?" he says, after he'd cracked one or two of them.

"Down on the slope of Green Bushes," says Mr. 'Coon. "Why, aren't they good ones?"

"I suppose they were once," says Mr. Squirrel—"two or three years ago. Nuts have to be fresh to be good."

"That's what I told him," says Mr. 'Possum; "but he said you wouldn't know the difference."

"Oh, he did, did he?" says Mr. Squirrel. "Well, I've got better nuts than these at home," and Mr. Squirrel he got up and left the table.

Then Jack Rabbit began.

"Where'd you get this salad?" he says, turning up his nose.

"Out by Mr. Man's back gate," says Mr. 'Possum. "Why, isn't it good?"

"Might have been once," says Mr. Rabbit. "I s'pose it's some Mr. Man threw out because it was wilted."

"That's what I told him," says Mr. 'Coon, "but he said you wouldn't know the difference."

"Oh, he did, did he? Well, I've got better salad than this at home," and Jack Rabbit he got up and he left the table.

And then, pretty soon, Mr. Turtle made a face over the fish because they were salt mackerel and not nice fresh fish, such as he was used to at home. So he got up and left the table, too, and there sat the 'Coon and 'Possum and the Old Black Crow all by themselves and looking cheap enough to fall through the floor. Mr. Crow said it wasn't his fault, and then Mr. 'Coon and Mr. 'Possum commenced to blame it on each other, and nearly got into a fight. They were just about to fight when Mr. Crow happened to think of something. Mr. Crow always did think of things.

"I'll tell you!" he says. "We'll just rent rooms."

"Do what?" says Mr. 'Possum and Mr. 'Coon together.

"Why, just rent each of our guests his room and let him take his meals out. Then we won't have any work."

"Whoo-ee!" says Mr. 'Possum and Mr. 'Coon both together, as loud as ever they could. That made all the guests come running back, and when they heard the new plan they all cheered, too, and said it was just the thing.

So then Mr. 'Possum went down and got the sign and brought it up and changed it to read:

THE HOLLOW TREE INN.

FURNISHED ROOMS ONLY.

And that was how business began at last in the Hollow Tree.

HOW UNCLE SILAS TRIED TO PLEASE AUNT MELISSY

Well, you remember that the Hollow Tree people took four of their friends to live with them and called it the Hollow Tree Inn. Mr. Robin came, and Mr. Turtle, also Jack Rabbit and Mr. Squirrel, and they made a jolly crowd after they got settled and knew about each getting his own things to eat, because the Hollow Tree people—the 'Coon and 'Possum and the old black Crow—found they couldn't suit their guests exactly when it came to a steady diet. So they all kept house together, and used to go out days (and nights, too, sometimes, when Mr. Man and Mr. Dog were tired and asleep and didn't want to be disturbed) and get nice things. Then they'd bring them in and fix them to suit themselves, and have them all on the big table down stairs, nice and comfortable, where they could sit and talk as long as they pleased.

It was a good deal like a big family when they were all together that way, and they used to say how nice it was, and once Mr. 'Possum said he always did think a big family was nice, anyway. Then Jack Rabbit laughed and said he should think Mr. 'Possum was just the kind of a man for a big family, being fond of good things to eat and not very fond of getting them for himself, and mostly fat and sleepy like. He said if there was just a nice, spry Mrs. 'Possum, now, to keep house and look after things he should think it would be ever so much better than living in bachelor quarters, or, rather, thirds, with Mr. 'Coon and Mr. Crow, and not having things very orderly. Of course, with himself, Jack Rabbit said, it was different, but even at his house it got lonesome, too, now and then.

Well, Mr. 'Possum thought a minute, and then he said that there was such a thing as folks being too spry, and that it was because he had always been afraid of getting that kind that he had been pretty well satisfied to live in the Hollow Tree just as he was. He said that he had once had an uncle that something happened to in that line, and whenever he thought about poor Uncle Lovejoy he didn't seem to care much about trying anything he wasn't used to. Then they all wanted him to tell about Uncle Lovejoy and what happened to him. So Mr. 'Possum did tell, and it went this way:

"Once upon a time," he said, "Uncle Lovejoy—we always called him Uncle Silas then, and he was uncle on my mother's side, and lived with Aunt Melissy in a nice place just beyond the Wide Pawpaw Hollows—once upon a time, as I was saying, he had to go to town on some business, and that was something that never happened to Uncle Lovejoy before."

"Well, Aunt Melissy was always a spry woman, as I said, and stirring—very stirring, and primpy, too. But she was never as stirring and spry and primpy as she was the day that Uncle Silas started for town. She dressed him all up neat and proper in his very best things, and tied his tie for him, and while she was tying it she says:

"'Now, Silas,' she says, 'when you get to town you buy a few little articles right away and put them on. You don't want folks to see that you come from the country, you know, and you don't want Cousin Glenwood to be ashamed of you before folks. Cousin Glen will know just what things you need and where to get them.' Then she told him not to get run over by anything, or blow out the gas, or let anybody see that he wasn't used to things, because, you see, Aunt Melissy was proud, being a Glenwood herself. Then Uncle Lovejoy promised all those things, and that he would use his napkin and not eat pie out of his hand or drink out of his finger bowl, and a lot more things that Aunt Melissy remembered at the last minute. So you see by the time he got on the train he had a good deal to think about, and he kept thinking about it until by the time he got to the city he'd made up his mind he'd try to do for once everything she told him to and give her a pleasant surprise with the way he had fixed up and improved his manners when he got back. Uncle Lovejoy was good natured and always anxious to please folks, especially Aunt Melissy."

"Well, Cousin Glenwood met him at the station, and about the first thing Uncle Silas said was to ask him where he got his clothes, and to tell him that Aunt Melissy had said he was to fix up, so's folks wouldn't think he came from the country, which, of course, she had. That just suited Cousin Glenwood, for he liked to spend money and show off what he knew about the city; so he took Uncle Lovejoy 'most everywhere, and told him to buy 'most everything he saw. And of course Uncle Silas did it, because he wanted to surprise Aunt Melissy when he got back and make her feel happy for once in her life."

"Cousin Glen took Uncle Lovejoy to the stores first, and then to a good many different kinds of places afterward, and every place where there was a mirror Uncle Lovejoy would stand before it and admire himself and wonder what Aunt Melissy would say when he got home. He kept buying new things every day, because every day he'd see somebody with something on or carrying or leading something, and when he remembered what Aunt Melissy said, he made up his mind he'd have to have all the things to please her, and he got them as far as he could. Even Cousin Glenwood had to commence buying things pretty soon to keep up, and before long people used to stop on the street and look at them when they went by. Uncle Silas didn't want to go home, either, when the time came, but of course he had to, and he put on his best clothes for the trip, and took a young man he'd hired to wait on him, and started.

"He didn't tell Aunt Melissy just what time he'd be there, so it was a surprise sure enough. He walked right into the yard, and behind was the young man he'd hired, carrying his things. Aunt Melissy was getting dinner, and had just come to the door a minute to see what time it was by the sun, when all of a sudden, as she looked up, there he was! He had his hat in one hand and a cane in the other, and was leading a game chicken by a string. All his boxes and bundles and the young man were behind him. Uncle Lovejoy wore an eyeglass, too, and smoked a paper thing he said was a cigarette. My little cousins, who were there, told me afterward that their pa had never looked so fine in his life before or since. They didn't know him at all, and neither did Aunt Melissy. She thought he was somebody with something to sell at first, and when he said:"

"'Aw, there, Melissah!' she threw up her hands and was just about to call for help, when just that minute she saw it was Uncle Silas.

"Poor Uncle Silas! He meant to surprise her, and he did it sure enough. He meant to please her, though, and he didn't do that worth a cent. It seemed funny, but she was mad. That's just the trouble about women folks; you never know when you're going to please them. My little cousins said they never saw their ma so mad before or since. She made Uncle Lovejoy take off all his nice clothes, and the young man, too, and she cooked the game chicken for dinner. Then, right after dinner, she picked up a bag of shinney sticks that Uncle Lovejoy had brought home, and she says to him and the young man:"

"'Now you get out in the garden,' she says, 'both of you, and try to earn back some of this money you've been spending.' And Uncle Lovejoy didn't feel very much like it, but he went, and so did the young man. So did Aunt Melissy, and she used up most of those shinney sticks on Uncle Silas and the young man before fall, and Uncle Silas never saw any of his nice clothes again, though they had the best garden they ever did have, so my little cousins said.

"And that," said Mr. 'Possum, leaning back in his chair to smoke, "that's why I've always been afraid to try family life. It's easier to please one than two, especially when the other one is a spry, stirring person like Aunt Melissy Lovejoy."

"What became of all the good clothes?" asked Jack Rabbit, who was always very stylish.

"Why, I've heard," said Mr. 'Possum, "that Aunt Melissy made some of them over for my little cousins, and that she traded off the rest of them to a pedler for patent medicine to give Uncle Silas for a weak mind, and I think he needed it some myself for trying to please her in the first place."

Mr. Rabbit nodded.

"It takes all kind of people to make a world," he said.

Mr. 'Coon yawned and rubbed his eyes. The others were fast asleep.

THE HOLLOW TREE POETRY CLUB

MR. CROW PLANS AN ENTERTAINMENT FOR THE FOREST PEOPLE

HAD TO SCRATCH HIS HEAD AND THINK PRETTY HARD.

Once upon a time, when it was getting along toward fall in the Hollow Tree where Jack Rabbit and Mr. Robin and the others had come to live with the 'Coon and 'Possum and the old black Crow, there began to be long evenings, and the Hollow Tree people used to think of new ways to pass the time. They tried games at first, and sleight of hand tricks. Then they tried doing things, and Mr. Turtle carried them all together twice around the big parlor room on his back. But even that wasn't so funny after the first evening, and Mr. Crow, who did most of the thinking, had to scratch his head and think pretty hard what to do next.

All at once he happened to remember that Jack Rabbit, who was the big man of the party, was also a first rate poet, and liked to read his own poetry better than anything. So, when he thought of that, he said:

"I'll tell you. We'll have a poetry club."

And of course that made Mr. Rabbit wake up right away.

"What's that?" he said. "What kind of a thing is a poetry club?"

POOR MR. DOG.

"Why," said Mr. Crow, "it's a place where the members each write a poem and read it at the next meeting. You're the only real, sure enough poet, of course, and will be president, and write the best poem, but the rest of us can try, and you can tell us our mistakes. I've heard that Mr. Man has them, and they're ever so much fun."

Jack Rabbit thought so, too, and all the others liked the plan. So they elected Mr. Rabbit president and then went to work on their poems. They couldn't have the first meeting very soon, for it took longer to write poems in those days than it does now, so before they got half ready the news got out some way, and even Mr. Dog had heard of it.

Poor Mr. Dog! It made him really quite ill to think he wasn't on very good terms with the Hollow Tree people, for he thought he could write pretty nice poetry, too, and he wanted to belong to that club worse than anything he could think of. He wanted to so bad that at last he told Mr. Robin that if they'd just let him come he'd promise anything they asked.

MR. RABBIT BOWED.

They didn't want to let him, though, until Mr. Crow, who always felt kind of sorry for Mr. Dog, said he didn't see why Mr. Dog shouldn't come and look in through the window shutters, and that they could nail a seat for him on a limb just outside. They could pull him up to it with a rope and he could sit there and listen and applaud the poems all through without being able to do any damage to the poets, and he would be glad enough to be let down by the time they got done reciting.

So they sent him an invitation, and Mr. Dog was as happy as a king. He went right to work on his poem, and he worked all night and walked up and down the yard all day trying to think up rhymes for "joyful" and "meeting," and a lot of other nice words. Even when he was asleep he dreamed about it, and said over some of the lines out loud and jerked his paws about as if he were reciting it and making motions. You see, Mr. Dog hadn't always done just right by the Hollow Tree people, and he was anxious to make a good impression and fix up things. He fixed himself all up, too, when the night came for the meeting, and took his poem under his arm and lit a cigar that he'd borrowed of Mr. Man for the occasion, and away he went.

The Hollow Tree people were on the lookout for him and had the rope down and ready. So Mr. Dog tied it around under his arms, and they pulled and pulled, and up he came. Then, when he got pretty close to the window, they closed the shutter and put the rope through and pulled him up still a little higher, so that he could reach the seat on the limb, which was fixed just right for him to sit there and lean on the window sill while he listened and looked in.

Of course, Mr. Dog wished he was inside, like the others, but he knew why he wasn't, and he was glad enough to be there at all. He peeked through the slats at the big room and smiled and said some nice things about how pretty the room looked, till they all got real sociable with him. Then Jack Rabbit called the meeting to order and made a few remarks.

109

He said the duties of his office had kept him from writing quite as long and as good a poem as he would have liked to write, but that he hoped they might be willing to hear what he had done. Then they all shouted, "Yes, yes!" and "Hear, hear!" and Mr. Rabbit bowed first to the ones inside and then to Mr. Dog outside, and began:

THE JOYS OF POETRY.

BY J. RABBIT.

Oh, sweet the joys of poetry
In the merry days of spring,
When the dew is on the meadow
And the duck is on the wing!
For 'tis then, from Dan to Dover,
I'm a rover 'mid the clover,
Seeking rhymes the country over
With a ring, sing, swing—
With a ding, dong, ding,
And a ting a ling a ling—
For I'm the rhyming rover of the spring.

Oh, sweet the joys of poetry
In the pleasant summer time!
For 'tis then I have no trouble
To compose my gentle rhyme;
In a nooklet by the brooklet
I can think up quite a booklet,
As with fishing line and hooklet
I assist the fish to climb
To the music of my chime,
For with rollick and with rhyme
I'm the poet of the pleasant summer time.

Oh, sweet the joys of poetry
When any days have come,
When the autumn zephyrs whisper
Or the winter breezes hum!
For 'tis then my thoughts unfurling,
While the smoke goes upward curling,
Come a whirling, swirling, twirling,
With a rumty, tumty, turn,
Come a twirling, swirling, whirling,
Like the rattle of a drum.
Come a whirling, come a swirling;
For in spring or in the summer,
In the autumn or the winter
I'm the rumty, tumty, tummer
That rejoices in the seasons as they come.

Well, when Mr. Rabbit got through everybody sat still for a minute, till Mr. Dog called out for somebody to come and unwind him so he could get his breath again. Then they all commenced to laugh and shout and pound on the table. And Mr. Rabbit coughed and looked pleased and said it was easy enough to do when you knew how.

LOOKED FOOLISH AND SWALLOWED TWO OR THREE TIMES.

Then Mr. 'Possum, who was next on the program, said he hoped they'd let him off this time because he could only think of four lines, and that he was a better hand at the dinner table than he was at poetry, anyway. But they wouldn't do it, so he got up and looked foolish and swallowed two or three times before he could get started.

WHAT I LOVE.

BY A. PUFFINGTON 'POSSUM.

I love the fragrant chicken pie
That blooms in early spring;
I love a chicken stew or fry,
Or any old thing.

Mr. 'Possum's poem was short, but it went right to the spot, and the way they applauded almost made Jack Rabbit jealous. He said that it was 'most too true to be good poetry, but that it was good for a first effort, and that being short helped it. Then Mr. Robin spoke his piece:

MOTHER AND ME.

BY C. ROBIN.

When the bud breaks out on the maple bough
Mother and me we build our nest—
A twig from the yard and a wisp from the mow
And four blue eggs 'neath the mother breast.

111

Up in the tree, mother and me,
Happy and blithe and contented are we.

When the daisies fall and the roses die,
An empty nest in the boughs to swing—
Four young robins that learn to fly
And a sweet adieu till another spring.
Then up in the tree, mother and me,
Happy once more and contented we'll be.

The applause wasn't so loud after Mr. Robin's poem, but they all said it was very pretty, and Mr. 'Possum even wiped his eyes with his handkerchief, because it made him remember something sad. Mr. Rabbit said that it ought to be "Mother and I," but that it didn't make much difference, he supposed, about grammar, so long as it rhymed and sounded nice. Then Mr. Crow got up.

JUST NOTHING.

BY J. CROW.

While others may sing of the pleasures of spring,
Or winter or summer or fall,
I'll sing not of these, because, if you please,
I'll sing of just nothing at all.
Just nothing at all, because, oh, ho!
I'll sing of myself, an old black crow.

As black as a coal and as homely as sin—
What more can I tell you, I pray?
For when you have nothing to sing of, why, then,
Of course there is nothing to say.
Nothing to say at all, oh, ho!
Except goodby to the old black crow—
The rollicking old black crow!

They made a good deal of fuss over Mr. Crow's poem. They applauded, of course, but they said it wasn't so at all, and that Mr. Crow was a good deal more than "just nothing." They said that it was he who had got up this party, and that he was the best man to plan and cook anywhere. Mr. 'Possum said he even liked Mr. Crow's April fool chicken pies, and then they all remembered and laughed, even to Mr. Crow himself. After that it was Mr. Squirrel's turn. Mr. Squirrel coughed twice and straightened his vest before he began, so they knew his poem wasn't to be funny.

THE FOOLISH LITTLE LAD.

BY MR. GRAY SQUIRREL.

Once on a time, the story goes,
A silly squirrel lad
One summer day did run away—
Which made his ma feel bad.

She hunted for him up and down
And round and round she ran—
Alas, that foolish squirrel boy
Was caught by Mr. Man.

For he had tried to climb a tree
As Mr. Man came past.
"I'll make you climb!" said Mr. Man,
And walked home pretty fast.

When he got there a boy came out
As Mr. Man went in.
That silly squirrel soon was put
Into a house of tin.

112

"Now you can climb!" said Mr. Man,
But when he did he found
That nice tin house, so bright and new,
Turned round and round and round.

And there he climbs and climbs all day
And never seems to stop,
And I have heard my mother say
He'll never reach the top.

When Mr. Squirrel sat down there wasn't a dry eye in the room, and even Mr. Dog outside was affected. He said he'd seen that poor little squirrel at Mr. Man's house turning and turning away in his tin wheel, and felt so sorry for him that two or three times he'd tried to get him out. He said, though, that Mr. Man had always caught him at it and that then they didn't get on well for a day or two. He was so tender-hearted, though, he said, that he couldn't help pitying the little fellow, climbing and climbing all day long and never getting anywhere. Mr. 'Possum shivered, and said it reminded him of bad dreams he'd had sometimes, when he'd eaten too much supper, and dreamed of climbing the rainbow. Then they all sat still and waited for Mr. Turtle, who came next.

MY SNUG HOUSE.

BY D'LAND TURTLE.

Oh, what do I care for your houses of wood,
Your houses of brick or of stone,
When I have a house that is cosy and good—
A beautiful house of my own?
And the doors will not sag and the roof will not crack
Of the house that I carry about on my back.

It is never too large and 'tis never too small,
It is with me wherever I roam.
In spring or in summer, in winter or fall,
I always can find my way home.
For it isn't so hard to remember the track
To the house that you carry about on your back.

Well, of course, everybody applauded that, and then it was Mr. 'Coon's time. Mr. 'Coon said he was like Mr. 'Possum. He wasn't much on poetry, and only had four lines. He said they were some like Mr. 'Possum's, too.

THE BEST THINGS.

BY Z. COON.

I like the spring, I like the fall,
I like the cold and heat,
And poems, too, but best of all
I like good things to eat.

113

LEANED OVER CLOSE TO THE BLINDS AND COMMENCED TO READ.

That brought the house down, and the Hollow Tree people thought the entertainment was over. They were going to have supper right away, but Mr. Dog called out to wait a minute. He said he had a little poem himself that he wanted to read. So out of politeness they all sat still, though they didn't expect very much. Then Mr. Dog unrolled his poem and leaned over close to the blinds and commenced to read.

MY FOREST FRIENDS.

BY MR. DOG.

Oh, dear to me my forest friends,
Especially Mr. Rabbit—
I love his poetry very much,
And every gentle habit.

And dear to me is Mr. 'Coon,
And also Mr. 'Possum;
I hope to win their friendship soon—
'Twill be a precious blossom.

And Mr. Crow and Robin, too,
With fancy sweet and fertile,
And Mr. Squirrel, kind and true,
And likewise Mr. Turtle.

Oh, dear to me my forest friends,
Especially Mr. Rabbit—
I love his poetry very much
And every gentle habit.

Before Mr. Dog was half through reading the Hollow Tree people had gathered around the window to listen. By the time he got to the end of the third stanza he had to stop for them to cheer, and when he read the last one, Jack Rabbit pounded on the shutter with his fist and shouted, "Hurrah for Mr. Dog! Hurrah for Mr. Dog!" just as loud as ever he could, while all the others crowded up and shouted and tried to pound, too.

Well, maybe the shutter wasn't very strong, or maybe they crowded and pounded too hard in their excitement over Mr. Dog's nice poem, for all at once there was a loud crack and the shutter flew open and out went Mr. Rabbit right smack into the arms of Mr. Dog!

I tell you that was pretty sudden and—Mr. Rabbit was scared. So were all the others and they were going to grab the shutter and close it again and leave Mr. Rabbit out there. But Jack Rabbit thinks quick.

"Oh Mr. Dog," he said, "that was the nicest poem I ever heard. Let me embrace you, Mr. Dog, and be your friend forever after!"

Then he hugged Mr. Dog just as tight as he could, and Mr. Dog hugged him, too, and shed tears, he was that happy. He had been wanting to make up with the forest people for a long time, but he hadn't expected this. Then the others all saw how it was and they shouted, "Hurrah for Mr. Dog!" again and invited him in. And Mr. Dog went in and they had the biggest supper and the biggest time that ever was known in the Hollow Tree.

And that's how Mr. Dog got to be friends with all the Hollow Tree people at last. And he stayed friends with them ever and ever so long—and longer—just as long as he lived, for the Mr. Dog that isn't good friends with them now isn't the same Mr. Dog. And he isn't as smart, either, for he can't write poetry, and he's never even been able to find the Hollow Tree, where the 'Coon and 'Possum and the old black Crow live together and every summer keep open house for their friends.

AROUND THE WORLD AND BACK AGAIN

Once upon a time, when Mr. Dog was over spending the evening with the Hollow Tree people, he told them that Mr. Man had said the world was round, like a ball. Of course this was after Mr. Dog got to be good friends with the 'Possum and the 'Coon and the old black Crow, and he often used to come over to the Hollow Tree, where they lived, for a quiet talk and smoke, and to tell the things that Mr. Man said, and did, and what he had on his table for dinner.

The Hollow Tree people liked to hear about Mr. Man, too; but when they heard what he said about the world being round they thought there must be some mistake in the way Mr. Dog had understood it. Mr. 'Coon said that it couldn't be so, for the edge of the world was just beyond the last trees of the big deep woods, and that he'd often sat there and hung his feet over and watched the moon come up. Mr. 'Possum said so, too; and Mr. Crow said that the other edge was over along the wide, blue water, where Mr. Turtle lived, and that of course the water was flat, as everybody could see. Anyway, it would spill out if it wasn't.

But Mr. Dog stuck to it that Mr. Man had said just what Mr. Dog had said he said, and that, what was more, Mr. Man had said that the world turned over every day, and that the sun and moon and stars all went round it. And Mr. Man had said, too, that people sometimes went around the world, and didn't turn over or fall off into the sky when they were underneath, but kept on, and came up on the other side, right back to the very place they started from.

Well, that made them all wonder a good deal more than ever; and Mr. Jack Rabbit, who came in just then for the evening, said he shouldn't be a bit surprised if it were true, for he'd often noticed how the seasons went round and round, and he thought, now, they must travel around the world some way, too. He said he'd composed some poetry on Spring as he came along, and that now he understood some lines of it better than he had at the start; for, of course, when poetry just comes to anybody, as it does to Mr. Rabbit, it isn't expected that even the poet himself will understand it very well at first.

Then they all wanted to hear Jack Rabbit's poem, and Mr. Rabbit said that it really wasn't just as he wanted it yet, but that if they wouldn't expect too much, he'd let them hear how it went, anyway.

WHICH WAY, SPRING?

By J. Rabbit.

O Spring,
Ho, Spring!
Whither do you go, Spring?
If I did but know. Spring,
I would go there, too.
Pray, Spring,
Say, Spring,
Whither and away, Spring?
I would start to-day, Spring,
If I go with you.

And Spring answers:—
"Why, sir,
I, sir,
Just go tripping by, sir—
If you did but try, sir,
You could go with me.
Follow,
Follow,
Over hill and hollow—
Where the bluebirds call, O,
I am sure to be."

Well, everybody applauded that, of course; and Mr. 'Coon said that for his part he was tired of cold weather, and that if to-morrow was a bright day, and anybody'd go with him, he'd start out at sunrise and follow Spring clear around the world. Then Mr. 'Possum said he'd go just to see whether Mr. Man was right or not, and Mr. Crow said he'd go, too. Mr. Rabbit wanted to go to prove some things in his poem, but he had to make a garden if it was a good day, and Mr. Dog had an engagement to dig moles for Mr. Man.

SET OUT IN HIGH SPIRITS.

So the next morning, bright and early, the three Hollow Tree people got up and started. They packed some lunch in a basket, so they wouldn't get hungry, in case they were gone all day, and set out in high spirits; for it was a beautiful morning in April, and they knew Spring had come at last.

They saw a bluebird up in a tree not far away, and they remembered what Mr. Rabbit's poem had said about following him over hill and hollow; so they went along in that direction, talking and whistling and singing, because they felt so good in the fresh morning sunlight.

And Mr. Bluebird hopped and whistled and flew along ahead, until, by-and-by, they came to where Mr. Fox lived.

"Where are you fellows going, so early?" called Mr. Fox.

"We're following Spring around the world," called back Mr. Crow; and then they told him all that Mr. Dog had said.

Then Mr. Fox looked very wise, for he didn't know if Mr. Dog was playing a trick on them, or if it were really true that the world was round and he hadn't heard of it. Anyway, he wasn't going to let on, so he said, "Why, of course! I knew that all the time. You just keep right on until you come to that big elm over yonder, and turn to the right. Anybody over there can show you the way." Then Mr. Fox coughed and went back into the house, but he made up his mind he wouldn't laugh until he had seen Mr. Dog and was sure it was all a joke. And the Hollow Tree people kept on to the elm tree, and, sure enough, there was Mr. Bluebird, hopping and whistling and flying on ahead, for he'd been listening to what Mr. Fox had told them.

So they hurried right along after him till they came to Mr. Wolf's place. Mr. Wolf was looking out of his door as they came by.

"Hello, you early birds!" he called. "Whose hen-roost you been after?"

Then they told him they weren't thinking of such things as that on a beautiful morning like this, but that they were following Spring around the world. And they told him all that Mr. Man had said to Mr. Dog, and what Mr. Fox had said, and about Jack Rabbit's poem. Mr. Wolf thought he'd better be wise, too, until he found out just how things were, so he said:—"Sure enough! That's a good plan. I'd go along if I had time. I know the way well. You just keep on till you come to that creek yonder, then cross and turn to the right, and after that any one can show you the way."

AND MR. CROW, HE SAYS, "WHY, IT IS OUR TREE!"

So away went the Hollow Tree people, and when they got to the creek, and crossed, and turned to the right, there was the bluebird again, hopping and whistling and dancing on ahead, just in the direction that Mr. Wolf had said to go. Then, pretty soon, Mr. 'Possum said he was hungry, so they sat down on some moss and ate their

119

lunch, and Mr. Bluebird came up close and sang to them till Mr. 'Possum went to sleep in the sun and took a little nap, while the 'Coon and the Crow put what was left back into the basket and got ready to go. Then Mr. 'Possum woke up and said he was sure they must be nearly around the world, for he'd just had a dream about catching a chicken with four legs and two heads, and he knew that must mean something good. So then they went on and the bluebird went ahead, until they came to a fine, big cave, where Mr. Bear lived.

Now Mr. Bear is very big and wise—at least he thinks he is—and he knew right away that Mr. Dog was just playing a joke on them, or at least he thought he did, so he said:—"Well, well! I supposed you fellows knew all that long ago. You don't mean to say, do you, that this is really your first time round? Why, I go round the world every spring and fall, and buy most of my things on the other side. You just follow this path till you come to a big black rock, and then turn to the right and keep straight ahead. You can't miss the way."

Then Mr. Bear went back in his cave, and laid down and rolled over and laughed to think what a big joke everybody was playing on the Hollow Tree people. But the Hollow Tree people kept right on, for they saw Mr. Bluebird still whistling and dancing on ahead; and by-and-by they came to the big black rock that Mr. Bear had mentioned, and turned to the right again as he had told them, to do. Then they walked and walked, and Mr. Bluebird hopped and skipped and whistled, until at last, just as they were all getting very tired and it was most night, they came to a big hollow tree in a deep woods; and Mr. 'Possum looked up and says,

"Why," he says, "this tree looks a good deal like our tree!"

And Mr. 'Coon he says, "Why, it's just like our tree!"

And Mr. Crow, he says, "Why, it is our tree!" for of course they'd turned to the right three times, which brought them right back where they started from, though they did not know it.

So then all at once they commenced to laugh and shout:—"We've done it! We've done it!

"We've followed Spring around the world,
According to the plan!
Hurrah for Mr. Rabbit!
And hurrah for Mr. Man!"

And the bluebird up in the branches whistled and danced and shouted, too; and Jack Rabbit and Mr. Dog came over pretty soon to see if they'd got home yet. And of course Mr. Rabbit was proud about the way his poem had turned out; and Mr. Dog he was proud, too, on Mr. Man's account. Then they all had a big supper, to celebrate, and by-and-by Mr. Rabbit and Mr. Dog went away arm in arm, singing Mr. Rabbit's poem to the moon; while the 'Coon and 'Possum and the old black Crow went to bed happy because they had followed Spring clear around the world, and hadn't got lost or tumbled off into the sky, but were home again safe and sound in the Hollow Tree.

CHRISTMAS AT THE HOLLOW TREE INN

THE STORY TELLER TOLD THE LAST HOLLOW TREE STORY ON CHRISTMAS EVE. IT WAS SNOWING OUTSIDE, AND THE LITTLE LADY WAS WONDERING HOW IT WAS IN THE FAR DEEP WOODS

Once upon a time, he said, when the Robin, and Turtle, and Squirrel, and Jack Rabbit had all gone home for the winter, nobody was left in the Hollow Tree except the 'Coon and 'Possum and the old black Crow. Of course the others used to come back and visit them pretty often, and Mr. Dog, too, now that he had got to be good friends with all the Deep Woods people, and they thought a great deal of him when they got to know him better. Mr. Dog told them a lot of things they had never heard of before, things that he'd learned at Mr. Man's house, and maybe that's one reason why they got to liking him so well.

HE TOLD THEM ALL ABOUT
SANTA CLAUS.

He told them about Santa Claus, for one thing, and how the old fellow came down the chimney on Christmas Eve to bring presents to Mr. Man and his children, who always hung up their stockings for them, and Mr. Dog said that once he had hung up his stocking, too, and got a nice bone in it, that was so good he had buried and dug it up again as much as six times before spring. He said that Santa Claus always came to Mr. Man's house, and that whenever the children hung up their stockings they were always sure to get something in them.

MR. CROW HE MADE HIMSELF A NEW PAIR ON PURPOSE.

Well, the Hollow Tree people had never heard of Santa Claus. They knew about Christmas, of course, because everybody, even the cows and sheep, know about that, but they had never heard of Santa Claus. You see, Santa Claus only comes to Mr. Man's house, but they didn't know that, either, so they thought if they just hung up their stockings he'd come there, too, and that's what they made up their minds to do. They talked about it a great deal together, and Mr. 'Possum looked over all his stockings to pick out the biggest one he had, and Mr. Crow he made himself a new pair on purpose. Mr. 'Coon said he never knew Mr. Crow to make himself such big stockings before, but Mr. Crow said he was getting old and needed things bigger, and when he loaned one of his new stockings to Mr. 'Coon, Mr. 'Coon said, "That's so," and that he guessed they were about right after all. They didn't tell anybody about it at first, but by and by they told Mr. Dog what they were going to do, and when Mr. Dog heard it he wanted to laugh right out. You see, he knew Santa Claus never went anywhere except to Mr. Man's house, and he thought it would be a great joke on the Hollow Tree people when they hung up their stockings and didn't get anything.

But by and by Mr. Dog thought about something else. He thought it would be too bad, too, for them to be disappointed that way. You see, Mr. Dog liked them all now, and when he had thought about that a minute he made up his mind to do something. And this is what it was—he made up his mind to play Santa Claus!

He knew just how Santa Claus looked, 'cause he'd seen lots of his pictures at Mr. Man's house, and he thought it would be great fun to dress up that way and take a bag of presents to the Hollow Tree while they were all asleep and fill up the stockings of the 'Coon and 'Possum and the old black Crow. But first he had to be sure of some way of getting in, so he said to them he didn't see how they could expect Santa Claus, their chimneys were so small, and Mr. Crow said they could leave their latch string out down stairs, which was just what Mr.

122

Dog wanted. Then they said they were going to have all the folks that had spent the summer with them over for Christmas dinner and to see the presents they had got in their stockings. They told Mr. Dog to drop over, too, if he could get away, and Mr. Dog said he would, and went off laughing to himself and ran all the way home because he felt so pleased at what he was going to do.

IT GOT HEAVIER AND HEAVIER.

Well, he had to work pretty hard, I tell you, to get things ready. It wasn't so hard to get the presents as it was to rig up his Santa Claus dress. He found some long wool out in Mr. Man's barn for his white whiskers, and he put some that wasn't so long on the edges of his overcoat and boot tops and around an old hat he had. Then he borrowed a big sack he found out there, too, and fixed it up to swing over his back, just as he had seen Santa Claus do in the pictures. He had a lot of nice things to take along. Three tender young chickens he'd borrowed from Mr. Man, for one thing, and then he bought some new neckties for the Hollow Tree folks all around, and a big, striped candy cane for each one, because candy canes always looked well sticking out of a stocking. Besides all that, he had a new pipe for each, and a package of tobacco. You see, Mr. Dog lived with Mr. Man, and didn't ever have to buy much for himself, so he had always saved his money. He had even more things than that, but I can't remember just now what they were; and when he started out, all dressed up like Santa Claus, I tell you his bag was pretty heavy, and he almost wished before he got there that he hadn't started with quite so much.

HE ALMOST HAD TO LAUGH RIGHT OUT LOUD.

It got heavier and heavier all the way, and he was glad enough to get there and find the latch string out. He set his bag down to rest a minute before climbing the stairs, and then opened the doors softly and listened. He didn't hear a thing except Mr. Crow and Mr. 'Coon and Mr. 'Possum breathing pretty low, and he knew they might wake up any minute, and he wouldn't have been caught there in the midst of things for a good deal. So he slipped up just as easy as anything, and when he got up in the big parlor room he almost had to laugh right out loud, for there were the stockings sure enough, all hung up in a row, and a card with a name on it over each one telling who it belonged to.

Then he listened again, and all at once he jumped and held his breath, for he heard Mr. 'Possum say something. But Mr. 'Possum was only talking in his sleep, and saying, "I'll take another piece, please," and Mr. Dog knew he was dreaming about the mince pie he'd had for supper.

So, then he opened his bag and filled the stockings. He put in mixed candy and nuts and little things first, and then the pipes and tobacco and candy canes, so they'd show at the top, and hung a nice dressed chicken outside. I tell you, they looked fine! It almost made Mr. Dog wish he had a stocking of his own there to fill, and he forgot all about them waking up, and sat down in a chair to look at the stockings. It was a nice rocking chair, and over in a dark corner where they wouldn't be apt to see him, even if one of them did wake up and stick his head out of his room, so Mr. Dog felt pretty safe now, anyway. He rocked softly, and looked and looked at the nice stockings, and thought how pleased they'd be in the morning, and how tired he was. You've heard about people being as tired as a dog; and that's just how Mr. Dog felt. He was so tired he didn't feel a bit like starting home, and by and by—he never did know how it happened—but by and by Mr. Dog went sound asleep right there in his chair, with all his Santa Claus clothes on.

TO SEE MR. DOG JUMP RIGHT STRAIGHT OUT OF HIS CHAIR.

And there he sat, with his empty bag in his hand and the nice full stockings in front of him, all night long. Even when it came morning and began to get light Mr. Dog didn't know it; he just slept right on, he was that tired. Then pretty soon the door of Mr. 'Possum's room opened and he poked out his head. And just then the door of Mr. 'Coon's room opened and he poked out his head. Then the door of the old black Crow opened and out poked his head. They all looked toward the stockings, and they didn't see Mr. Dog, or even each other, at all. They saw their stockings, though, and Mr. 'Coon said all at once:—

"Oh, there's something in my stocking!"

And then Mr. Crow says:—"Oh, there's something in my stocking, too!"

And Mr. 'Possum says:—"Oh, there's something in all our stockings!"

And with that they gave a great hurrah all together, and rushed out and grabbed their stockings and turned around just in time to see Mr. Dog jump right straight up out of his chair, for he did not know where he was the least bit in the world.

"Oh, there's Santa Claus himself!" they all shouted together, and made a rush for their rooms, for they were scared almost to death. But it all dawned on Mr. Dog in a second, and he commenced to laugh and hurrah to think what a joke it was on everybody. And when they heard Mr. Dog laugh they knew him right away, and they all came up and looked at him, and he had to tell just what he'd done and everything; so they emptied out their stockings on the floor and ate some of the presents and looked at the others, until they almost forgot about breakfast, just as children do on Christmas morning.

Then Mr. Crow said, all at once, that he'd make a little coffee, and that Mr. Dog must stay and have some, and by and by they made him promise to spend the day with them and be there when the Robin and the Squirrel and Mr. Turtle and Jack Rabbit came, which he did.

And it was snowing hard outside, which made it a nicer Christmas than if it hadn't been, and when all the others came they brought presents, too. And when they saw Mr. Dog dressed up as Santa Claus and heard how he'd gone to sleep and been caught, they laughed and laughed. And it snowed so hard that they had to stay all night, and after dinner they sat around the fire and told stories. And they had to stay the next night, too, and all that Christmas week. And I wish I could tell you all that happened that week, but I can't, because I haven't time. But it was the very nicest Christmas that ever was in the Hollow Tree, or in the Big Deep Woods anywhere.

And this, said the Story Teller, is the very last Hollow Tree story, and there will be no more, for they all came out through Mr. Dog, and Mr. Dog has gone away now into that Far Land of Evening where all good dogs go to when they get very, very old. He was friends with the Hollow Tree people to the last, and when he got too old to visit them, they used to come to see him, sometimes at night, when Mr. Man was asleep. And when Mr. Dog went away on his long journey beyond the sunset they were all so sorry, for they knew that no other Mr. Dog would ever be friends with them, and they were very sad in the Hollow Tree for a long time.

Then here's goodby to the old black Crow,
And the rest, with a one, two, three!
And here's goodby to the Hollow, Hollow, Hollow—
Good-by to the Hollow Tree.

GOOD-BYE TO THE LITTLE LADY

WHAT SHE WISHES AND WHAT THE STORY TELLER SAYS

The Little Lady looks into the fire thoughtfully.

"And isn't there any more about the Hollow Tree?" she says at last.

The Story Teller looks into the fire, too.

"I'm afraid not," he answers.

"And won't you never know any more? Not ever—in a thousand days?"

"I—no, I'm afraid not."

"I wish we lived in a Hollow Tree," says the Little Lady.

From the House of Many Windows the Story Teller looks down on the dazzling lights and the clatter and jangle of the street. Then he remembers cool, musky ways in the dim woods, down which the padded feet of the forest people pass silently to hidden homes of peace. The Story Teller sighs.

"Yes, sweetheart," he says, "I have wished that sometimes, too."

THE END

Made in the USA
Columbia, SC
16 March 2021